DOUBLE BLIND

A DANGEROUS EIGHT NOVEL

SLOANE SAVAGE

Copyright © 2019 by Sloane Savage (Heather Smith)

Publisher: Wild Fey, LLC/Heather Smith

All rights reserved.

This is a work of fiction. The characters, incidents, and dialogues in this book are of the author's imagination and are not to be construed as real. Any resemblance to actual events or persons, living or dead, is completely coincidental.

No part of this book may be reproduced in any form or by any electronic or mechanical means, including information storage and retrieval systems, without written permission from the author, except for the use of brief quotations in a book review.

Cover design by Damonza

damonza.com

Editing Services Provided by

Tawdra Kandle at tawdrakandle.com

John Robin's Team at storyperfectediting.com

PROLOGUE

Jayda

Two days ago...

Ana was livid. Jayda thought the bitch should be happy she was still breathing. Instead, Ana was ranting and raving over the family hierarchy and the typo on her new fake ID. Jayda had been sitting in the hotel suite for an hour already waiting to get final instructions about Saturday's hit. Ana had been on the phone most of that time yelling at underlings and hotel staff.

Jayda didn't understand what the deal was. It wasn't like Ana didn't have all the money she could spend in ten lifetimes. No matter the outcome of who controlled the Ivanov clan, Ana would inherit her father's wealth, which included complete control of two trusts the old man had set up for her son, Demitri. Like Ana's father, Mikhail, her son was now conveniently dead. He and Mikhail were both gunned down during the FBI standoff with the Ortega Cartel. The same event that almost killed Jayda's beloved Evgeni.

Evgeni was like a father to Jayda. She trusted him completely.

Ana was pissed at Evgeni as well, but Jayda wasn't exactly clear about those details. Was she pissed because Evgeni survived? She'd shown no emotion over her father and son's deaths, but Ana was one nested doll away from a full set—especially where empathy was concerned.

"I am my father's successor, not Nikolai," Ana yelled into the phone. "Nick betrayed the family. Father disowned him. I will be the new Tzar."

Jayda had to stop herself from laughing. The *Tzarina* was in rare form tonight.

Jayda's phone buzzed. It was a text from an unknown number.

UNKNOWN: New number, E

Ah, it was from Evgeni. Jayda updated her contacts, then texted back.

JAYDA: Hello my sweet. It is good to hear from you

Ana screeched with anger, causing Jayda to look up from her seat on the sofa.

"I told you I would be back in three weeks. I have things to finish up here before I'm able to return," Ana yelled.

Jayda watched as Ana listened to the caller. Ana's eyes narrowed as if the news were very, very bad.

Ana's demeanor changed. She stood straighter as if she were queen and her word was law.

"Ilya," Ana said, her voice as cool and sharp as a knife, "you have been loyal to me. That will not be forgotten. But I wish for a message to be sent to the others. I wish for them to know that I will not stand for any talk of revolt. My father left me in charge. Had he wanted Nick to run the family he would've never thrown him out. Do you understand me?"

Jayda had only met Ilya once, assuming it was the Ilya that had worked for Ana's father. Jayda didn't like him. He was a sniveling suck-up.

Ana's conversation continued. "Who is your best man? The man no one would suspect of being disloyal?"

Jayda, who was trying her best to remain invisible during Ana's tirade, glanced over at Fedor, the Ivanov clan guard who had remained behind as Ana's bodyguard. Where was Ana going with this?

"Kill him. Make sure the others know it was because there was the barest hint of disloyalty. I want all of them to think, 'if Sasha can be eliminated, anyone can.' Am I being clear?"

Fedor's jaw tightened, not that Ana noticed. He, like everyone else, respected Sasha. Jayda didn't know many of the lieutenants personally, but even she'd met Sasha. He was their most loyal man. Ana was an idiot for ordering his death.

Jayda's phone chirped, pulling her attention away from Ana. It was a reply from Evgeni.

EVGENI: Are you working for Ana?
JAYDA: Yes, why do you care?
EVGENI: Ana is the viper that killed my family

Jayda didn't understand. If Ana was responsible for Evgeni's family's death, then why would he continue to take jobs from her? Jayda replied to the text.

JAYDA: You have always worked for her
EVGENI: I had no fucking choice, but I will make her pay
JAYDA: Should I kill her for you?
EVGENI: Would you?
JAYDA: For double the fee
EVGENI: Acceptable. When?
JAYDA: Not now. I must finish prior commitments first.
 1-2 weeks

Jayda owed Evgeni everything for saving her. She would take care of Ana for him. The bitch was getting on Jayda's nerves anyway, plus Jayda thought perhaps Nikolai would also pay to have Ana taken care of. Jayda was not one to pass up a prime opportunity to make money. She just needed a way to contact Nikolai, then final arrangements could be made.

Evgeni texted back.

EVGENI: Agreed
JAYDA: BTW, Ana has just ordered Ilya to kill Sasha as a show of power and loyalty
EVGENI: Fucking hell, that bitch. I will attempt to intercede
JAYDA: Only two others know of this plan
EVGENI: You won't be burned, do not worry
JAYDA: Later my sweet

"Are you listening to me?" Jayda heard Ana's voice just before a hand slapped her across the face.

"Fucking hell," Jayda cursed. "What was that for?" Jayda rubbed her cheek where the sting of Ana's hand still lingered.

"Pay attention when you are in my presence," Ana said.

Lowering her hand, Jayda inclined her head. "Yes, ma'am. I am at your service."

"No interrogation of Ryker, just finish him."

"As you wish. What about Greyson?"

"I don't want them killed too close together. Next Thursday for Greyson. I'll plan to leave on Tuesday," Ana said.

Ana was an idiot. It was Thursday now. The Ryker kill was scheduled for Saturday night. To kill Greyson next Thursday would only separate the hits by five days—did Ana not understand that anything less than a week would be considered close? Evgeni would have waited for the first kill before making a decision on the second, which would allow him to incorporate any fallout from the first assignment into his plans for the second. Jayda considered suggesting the same strategy to Ana, but did Ana's opinion still matter?

Jayda would contact Nikolai. She'd offer her services, possibly even take out everyone before Ana left town. A coup. Evgeni would have his revenge and Ana would be paid twice for killing the same heartless bitch. She'd handle Greyson on Monday, then get Ana to transfer her payment, then kill Ana before she had a chance to leave the country. Yes, that would work out nicely.

With that decision made, Jayda turned her attention to the Ryker case. She needed to finalize her prep. At least now she didn't have to seduce him, but she still had to dye her hair red. Jayda fucking hated red. It never washed out well from her naturally blonde hair. She inevitably wound up with pink hair for three days. But in this case, she had no choice. Ryker had requested an escort with red hair, and a blue dress, and some other fucking shit about being a professor. The guy was a freak.

Jayda caught a movement out of the corner of her eye. Raising her hand, she blocked Ana's attempt to slap her again.

"I told you to pay attention," Ana said.

Jayda smiled. "Less than a week might be too close. I recommend—"

"I don't pay you to recommend. I pay you to kill people. When I say it's time, it's time. Do you have an understanding of your role now?"

"Yes, ma'am. I'll take care of it," Jayda said, as she imagined all the different ways she could kill Ana without even leaving her seat.

1

KAT

This is stupid—or brilliant, Kat thought as she made her way toward the restaurant. Stupid, because no one does blind dates anymore. Brilliant, because if this worked she'd finally be pulled from her rut of inaction. It wasn't like she had agoraphobia, but dating had become such a chore.

"My offer still stands, babe. I'm here for you," Rip said, his voice silky-smooth through Kat's Bluetooth earbud.

Kat rolled her eyes. Rip was her best friend. They'd been inseparable since they were six and he pulled her hair on the playground in first grade. They'd dated in high school, and Kat was fairly sure he'd take a bullet for her, but the chemistry for a real romantic relationship just wasn't there. They were each other's first, but the night they did it was the night Rip confessed he liked boys, too, and the way he talked about his crush on the school quarterback told her everything she needed to know.

Kat would never be his one and only, which was a shame, because he was drop-dead gorgeous and wicked smart. Every girl's dream, right?

She sometimes thought about what could have been. It wasn't like she'd picked out their china pattern, but they were from a small town in Illinois. It was just—you know—expected. They were supposed to go to college, then get married and have kids, raise a family, and grow old in the same town as their parents. That's just the way it was supposed to work.

Kat heard Rip sigh, bringing her attention back to their conversation.

"Kit-Kat, what are you thinking about?" he asked.

That you're gay, unavailable, and broke my heart, she thought, but didn't say. Instead, she said, "That this date is going to suck."

"Babe, I'm here for you."

She sighed. "Yes, I know you're willing to give it another try. Yes, I know you've significantly improved your technique. But I want a guy that will make my unrealistic romance novel fantasies come true. Sorry, big boy, that isn't you."

He laughed.

"Don't laugh. You may look the part, mister, but we both know you'd rather be with that romance novel fantasy, too. I can't…" Kat trailed off. She refused to get all sappy and emotional and say *I can't wait for you to wake up and decide you really do like girls better*—neither of them would be happy with that lie. He was the sexiest thing she'd ever laid eyes on—heck, they still cuddled in his bed some nights. He was her dependable, drama-free guy friend.

He was the reason she made it through all the losers that had darkened her door since they moved to New York City. And they weren't losers because Kat was picky. She had standards, of course, but honestly—who thought going skydiving was a good first date? Or the guy that wanted her to hop on the back of his Ducati—no, thank you. It wasn't like she wouldn't take risks, within reason, but come on—professional sky writers shouldn't even be a thing, much less a dating option. And let's not forget Frank, Mr. I-Love-To-Go-Camping-With-A-Utility-Knife-And-My-Wits, or Joe, Mr. Let's-Go-To-The-Gun-Range-And-Shoot-An-AK47-For-Fun. It was like Kat attracted these crazy—okay, dangerous—guys. She wanted Mr. Uncomplicated—a nice, safe driver, future white-picket-fence, with no specialty certifications for things that require extra insurance, kind of guy. She wanted a Rip that liked girls. Was that too much to ask?

"Kit-Kat, you know I love you, babe," he said, and she knew he meant it.

That's why Kat was out on this blind date, waiting to meet her first Mr. Right Wannabe and praying he wouldn't be a jackass. Ugh, this just wasn't her, but it needed to be her or she'd never find anyone.

"Rip, I just..."

"No worries, babe. I understand," Rip said. "Okay, so Plan B—Blind Dating Service. You're sure this isn't a service to find dates for the blind?"

Kat exhaled in exasperation. He just chuckled.

They'd been over this several times. It wasn't called Blind Dating Service. It was called NYC Blind Date. Its motto was 'What have you got to lose?' He just wanted to pull her chain.

"Okay, so you have your rules?" he asked.

"What rules?" she said in a panic.

"Kit-Kat," he admonished in that overly protective tone. "No going home with him."

"Absolutely not," she agreed. Kat took another deep breath. *Oh, God, I might throw up.*

"Breathe," he said, "and chill out. It's not like the last boy you slept with turned gay or anything."

Kat gasped. "That's not funny!" she mock scolded. He was trying to lighten the mood. And he wasn't the last guy she'd slept with, but Kat wasn't going there either.

"Protect the lady garden at all cost."

"Stop," she said, trying not to laugh. "Don't you dare repeat Sister Mary Margaret's sex ed talk. You'll jinx me."

He chuckled, which made her chuckle too.

In his best pep talk voice, he said, "Okay, babe, you got this. It's one blind date. You can do it."

"Yes. I can do this," Kat whispered as she opened the door to the restaurant and walked up to the hostess stand.

"You again?" the snooty hostess of Byron's Bistro said.

"Um…" Kat stammered. "I just walked in. I'm meeting a guy here. My name is Kat—Kaitlyn Fox."

Ms. Snooty Hostess looked Kat up and down. "Oh, you're not her. You can wait in the bar." She flicked her hand, as if saying *move along*.

"Thanks," Kat said, just as Rip said, "Bitch," in her ear.

"Whatever," Ms. Snooty groused, impatiently shooing Kat away.

"Ignore the harpy," Rip said.

"Right," Kat muttered, heading for the bar. "Ignore the fact that she said *whatever* like she meant *loser*. Ignore the fact that she's five-foot-ten in those killer heels and has boobs the size of a Hooter's waitress. And her long straight blonde hair probably makes every guy in this place drool. Oh, God," Kat gasped. "I should have worn my hair down."

"Kit-Kat, ignore the bitch. The hair is fine. You could have maybe picked the red dress."

"Oh, God, what's wrong with my dress?"

"Nothing. Chill out. You're perfect. You've got a rocking bod, and that Hooter's flunky sounds top heavy."

"Yeah, my five-foot-eight boy body is really what all the guys want," she sighed.

"Kit-Kat, we've talked about this. You have a rocking bikini body with enough up top to keep any man happy—I know, I've seen them, remember."

Kat laughed. "You don't count."

Okay, so her body wasn't that bad. She had some curves, but not many. Kat really did rock a bikini—not that she ever wore one anymore—sun damage was a thing. OMG. She really needed to get out more, which was why she was here. Frumpy dress and all.

"Quit putting yourself down, Kit-Kat. You rock and any guy would be lucky to have you," he said.

Kat glanced around. She wanted to sit at the bar, but there were no empty seats. She spotted the sign for the restroom. "Radio silence—I'm going in." This was their code phrase for heading to the can.

"My lips are sealed, babe. Don't forget to flush."

"Stop." Kat whispered.

"Watch it," a female voice said, shoulder checking Kat as she walked by.

Startled, Kat stepped aside. The rude woman glanced back over her shoulder. Kat was shocked. She could have been looking at her twin.

With a sneer, the woman's eyes took in Kat from head to toe. "This is the last time I wear something off the rack," she said.

As her words registered, Kat realized they were wearing the same dress. Other than the woman's obviously dyed red hair, they were carbon copies. The clone's hair was even twisted into a messy updo. Weird.

Rip broke the silence. "Who was that?"

"My doppelgänger. Except her hair's fake."

"Ignore her. You're there to meet Mr. Blind Right Now."

"Radio silence," she whispered, ignoring his bad joke. Muttering, she added, "I don't want to wind up an old maid."

Rip laughed. "Kit-Kat, you're twenty-three, not thirty. You live in NYC with a totally hot guy that loves you, and all the time in the world to find the white picket fence."

"Radio silence," she hissed, "or I'm hanging up."

He knew it annoyed her when people talked on their phone in the restroom. As Kat took care of business, she thought about what he had said. He was right, she was too young to worry about the white picket fence, and he was a totally hot guy that loved her

—just not in that way. She could do this—one blind date wouldn't kill her. She needed to take a few more risks—not skydiving on the first date risks—but something a little more spontaneous than a two-page LifePlanner spread for this week's packed lunch options. She was eating out on Monday. She'd just decided to do that. Fuck—that's still planning. Gah, spontaneity was hard.

As she left the stall, Rip blurted, "Just make sure he suits up."

Kat coughed out a laugh, causing the three women at the sinks to turn and look at her. Mortified, she quickly washed up and left. "We really need to discuss the rules of radio silence. And I'm not going home with him."

Rip laughed. "Okay, I'll see you in the morning. Love you, babe."

"I'll see you tonight." Kat growled, but she wasn't really mad.

"Oh, yes," he said seductively, "and will you wear the Princess Leah slave girl T-shirt I bought for you?"

"No! Goodbye, pervert." Kat ended the call, snagging her earring as she plucked the earbud out of her ear.

Straightening the little diamond stud, she tossed her earbud into her clutch, before she returned to the bar.

Kat scanned for a seat. Score, someone had just stood to leave. Kat's doppelgänger was MIA, so at least she wouldn't have to run into her again. Kat didn't need the rude woman's cold eyes shooting daggers at her while she waited.

2

BISHOP

"Screw you, Madeline. I know how to do my job," Bishop said, trying to keep his voice low and avoid attention from passersby on the street.

"Not according to the reports I've read," she said. "You're a loose cannon, Scott. I took a risk choosing you for this assignment."

Bishop sighed. She wasn't completely wrong. He'd royally fucked up his perfect record in Chicago when he tried to help his friend Drake's girlfriend out of a jam. Problem was, Drake's girl, Haden, was mixed up with both the Ivanov clan of Russian oligarchs and the Ortega drug cartel. The takedown didn't go smoothly, and Drake had shown up at the scene, almost screwing up the whole operation.

Because of that fuck up, Bishop had been loaned to the New York City FBI field office. An agent he'd gone through the academy with had requested him for the temporary assignment. The agent, Madeline "Mad Max" Maxwell, had recently been promoted into a role Bishop normally held. His new assignment wasn't a demotion per se, but she certainly made it feel that way.

But the op and his lower status weren't the only issues. Two years ago, Madeline and he had hooked up at an academy training exercise, something he wasn't sure her boss, NYC Assistant Director in Charge Reece Patterson, was aware of. Bishop had discussed the issue with his boss, Chicago ADIC Frazier Wilson. Wilson saw the assignment as a chance for Bishop to lay low while the Chicago investigation wound down. Bishop assured his boss that he had no intention of rekindling an affair that was long dead. They both agreed not to inform Patterson.

Even after the parameters of the assignment changed, Bishop's past involvement with Madeline had no chance of derailing Bishop's duties. Madeline and he were both professionals with an eye on career advancement, not a quickie in a surveillance van. Madeline's star was finally rising at the NYC office. She couldn't afford to fuck things up by screwing around with Bishop.

"Madeline, if you think you can find another dead ringer for West, then by all means do, and I'll go back to Chicago."

Madeline laughed. "You and I both know you need to finish this op or you might not have a job to return to. You lost a lot of ground, Scott. You and I both need this win, so get with the program."

"I'm not working against you. I've run dozens of ops like this. I know what I'm doing."

"This is my op, Scott. You follow my lead."

"It's your operation," Bishop conceded, "but you must let me do my job."

"Your job is to screw a hooker while I interrogate the real Ryker West. Stop overthinking it."

Bishop pinched the bridge of his nose. Technically he was going to the restaurant, Byron's Bistro, to meet a high-end escort. A *perk*, Cameron Greyson, president and CEO of Cameron Greyson Holdings, had insisted West accept as a prerequisite for them doing business. CGH was suspected of laundering money for its wealthy overseas clients, but so far the FBI had no proof.

Bishop was initially brought in to assist with surveillance only.

Madeline had informed him of the change in priorities during their briefing yesterday. Bishop would now be taking a new client meeting with Cameron Greyson. Greyson was scheduled to meet Ryker West, a financial advisor for Vasili Volkov. Volkov was rumored to control a third of the Russian black market. Bishop's priorities were changed when a picture of West was confused with a picture of Bishop with a beard. If not for West's beard, they could have been twins.

Of course, none of this mattered, until Madeline got lucky and hit on an old warrant from ten years ago. Ryker James West was wanted in Texas for failure to appear in court. It was little more than a traffic summons, but it gave Madeline the authority to have TSA detain him for arrest.

Bishop had spent the last twenty-four hours absorbing everything he could about West and Volkov. There wasn't much intel, but he'd memorized all there was. Madeline had sprung the date with the escort on him last minute, but it wasn't like he needed to prep for a paid companion. It would give him a chance to play Ryker West for real before he was scheduled to meet Greyson tomorrow.

All Bishop had to do was pass the escort test, then get Greyson to offer him a deal to launder money for the consortium.

The swap had gone off without a hitch. West had been quietly picked up from the airport this afternoon by Madeline, allowing Bishop to walk out of the airport as Ryker West.

So far, as West, Bishop had checked into his hotel—a CGH property—ordered room service, and sent word via the hotel's concierge that he'd see Greyson Sunday mid-morning for brunch as scheduled.

"My job's a bit more complicated than screwing the escort, which I don't plan to do," Bishop said, annoyed she'd even suggest it. "Have you had any luck with West so far?"

She ignored his question. "You've practiced the accent, correct?"

Bishop had been practicing non-stop since he got the assignment. It wasn't perfect, but it would pass. "Yes."

"And you received the dossier on your escort, correct?"

"Dossier, right. Yeah, I got the email with West's call girl specs."

"And you've studied them?" Madeline asked.

"You do realize the man ordered a submissive call girl, right, not a world class scholar looking to discuss quantum physics?" Bishop asked.

"As I remember, you were well versed in vanilla sex. I'm not sure I'd call you a connoisseur of the submissive arts."

Holy God. *Did she really just say that?* "He likes dominating demure women with red hair. It's not even all that kinky."

"Just make sure—"

"For fuck's sake Madeline. I'm not planning to sleep with her, but if I were, I've got this."

"Fine, just don't forget to pay her," she said, ending the call abruptly.

Bishop just stared at the phone. Was she trying to piss him off? Being riled up by Madeline before going in to the restaurant to find his paid escort wouldn't help him get into character. Slipping the phone back into his pocket, Bishop shook off Madeline's bad vibes. He knew his job, and he wouldn't forget about the money. Even though the girl's fee was paid by Greyson, the FBI might need leverage if she turned out to be somehow connected to the money laundering. With the extra payment they could bring her up on prostitution charges, without it, she was just a date.

"Dossier," he muttered, as he crossed the street.

The high-end bistro was busy. The glass windows along the front of the building showed the bar inside. He scanned the area for a redhead in a blue dress but didn't see anyone matching that description.

Entering, he bypassed the hostess and headed for the bar. Surveying the crowd, he spotted his date coming out of the restroom.

She was gorgeous. Not as flashy as he'd expected. Not that he'd ever hired an escort before, but he'd expected a woman so polished and primped she'd look fake. This woman was beautiful, but young. According to the email, West had requested a twenty-nine-year-old professor type with red hair. There was no way this girl was pushing thirty. She probably still got carded for drinks.

He watched as she found a seat at the bar.

Straightening his shoulders, he donned a more dominant persona. It was time for Ryker West to come out and play.

3

KAT

Kat was getting nervous. It was ridiculous. This was one blind date. What could possibly go wrong?

"Get you anything?" the bartender asked.

Kat was about to say no, then she remembered she'd decided to be more spontaneous. Hell yes, she was having a drink. Okay, a water, that was a drink. Before she could order, Kat felt a strong hand grab her elbow. Startled, she immediately thought of the self-defense moves Rip had been showing her last weekend. She prepared her one and only practiced move, which consisted of stomping on the stranger's instep, but was thrown off balance when Mr. Grabby-Hands spun her around on the stool to face him.

Ohmygod, she thought as she took in the golden god before her. He was more beautiful than Rip.

"Hello, gorgeous," he said in a sexy as hell British accent. "You're perfect. Exactly what I ordered."

"Umm...I'm Kat," Kat stupidly said, unable to form a coherent thought. Wait, what did he say? Goosebumps rushed across her arm as he rubbed the pad of his thumb over the skin at her elbow.

The hairs on the back of her neck stood on end. What the hell was this guy doing using a dating service? *Maybe he has a job that takes up all of his time—or he's a serial killer. Stop it, he's not a serial killer.*

"You're not a serial killer, right?" Kat said, before she could stop myself.

He chuckled. His laugh was deep and rumbling and made Kat want to sink into him.

Kat wanted to run her hands all over his lightly tanned skin. His gray eyes sparkled and the lights in the bar danced off his sexy just-out-of-bed hair.

Before she realized what she was doing, Kat reached up to touch those gorgeous blond locks. He caught her hand in his, a quizzical look on his face. Oh God, she was being crazy. Great, she'd come full circle. The guy was perfect and she was the whack-a-doodle—or was this just being assertive? Maybe he liked assertive.

Kat swallowed, her mouth suddenly dry. She needed to slow down. Unplanned didn't mean impetuous. She couldn't just jump this guy in the restaurant. Kat had to show restraint, right?

He tugged at her elbow, pulling her off the bar stool. Kat's legs buckled, but he caught her. His strong arms cradled her close.

"Easy, beautiful. I've got you," he said.

Kat had never understood what anyone meant by the expression *sex on legs*. Until now. Mr. Too-Good-To-Be-True was so panty dropping delicious it made her toes curl. Okay, she needed a drink. Kat turned back toward the bar.

"Oh, no, love," he said. "You may have already had one too many."

Kat opened her mouth to say she'd just needed some water—which was a total lie—when her eyes locked with his and she honestly almost had an orgasm just thinking about fucking this man. Clearly Kat and her battery-operated-boyfriend needed less together time, because real tactile interaction with another human was more than her sex deprived body could handle. When she got home, the B.O.B. was hitting the door.

Mr. Perfect led her away from the bar.

"Why the hell do you need a service to find a date?" she asked.

He chuckled, confirming that she'd just said that out loud.

Before she could apologize, he said, "How else would I get exactly what I'm looking for?"

Kat laughed. If he weren't so cute, and if this wasn't a prearranged blind date, she'd have questioned his cheesy pick-up line response.

Mr. Perfect caressed her arm, sending another zing of pleasure over her body.

Okay, Kat, you really need to pull it together. But this guy's touch was like some magic drug to her hoo-ha. God, she needed to get laid. Clearly being risk averse wasn't working for her. She should have taken Rip up on his offer. Maybe then she wouldn't be so take-me-I'm-yours near this guy.

Kat inhaled deeply. He even smelled good. Manly and fresh, like spring rain and summer. It was refreshing, since being this close to most guys would have been making her eyes water from their overuse of cologne.

She put her hand on his arm. The fabric of his tailored suit was buttery soft against her palm. She tugged for him to release her. His touch was making it hard for her to stay focused. They were supposed to be getting to know each other. Of course, impromptu Kat was ready to say "your place or mine." Kat couldn't let her off the chain yet.

"Should we get a table?" she asked.

"If we must," he said.

Kat's mouth hung open. No, she couldn't give in to her baser needs just yet. She had to get to know Mr. Sexy, before she let him have his way with her. Okay, this was why Kat didn't do impulsive. It was like once she'd decided to throw caution to the wind, she was ready to ride the tornado.

Holy fuck, Kat thought, putting her hand over her eyes. She really sucked at this. And why the hell couldn't she just attract a boring accountant? Accountants were safe. Mr. Sexy looked like he could win People's Man of the Year award. And there was no way that combination wouldn't lead to something dangerous.

Mr. Sexy lifted her chin and forced her to look at him. Why the hell did she have to get the lottery win of blind dates? Condoms made things safe, right?

"You seem nervous, love. Don't worry, I won't bite—hard."

Fucking hell. Did he know Kat was on the verge of agreeing to anything? She wasn't the kind of girl that did one-night stands normally, but she was Ms. Spontaneity tonight—maybe. Whatever, she was on the pill—to regulate her period, but that counts. She'd agreed to this ridiculous idea so she wouldn't die a born again virgin, right? And here was Mr. Golden-God-Of-My-Dreams propositioning her for sex. That really didn't sound safe, but it wasn't skydiving. She could do this.

Kat smiled, not sure what to say. She sucked at dating. She never seemed to attract the guys that made her want to beg for it. Thrill seekers that scared her, sure, but not gods among men. Of course, that was before she decided to take a risk and let shit happen.

It was ironic really. She'd not had overly high hopes tonight would be any different than her usual. Then Mr. I-Can't-Believe-His-Online-Profile-Name-Is-Gandalf-22 shows up and all bets were off.

"Lead the way," he said, pulling Kat from her spiraling out of control wet dreams.

Take a deep breath. Pull your shit together or he will put you in the crazy bucket and leave while you're in the restroom. Kat had to dial back the unconstrained sexy thoughts. She just needed to be herself—that's what all the online quizzes said anyway.

Mr. Sexy held her chair out for her to sit. The waiter took their drink order and left them with menus.

Kat took in the room. The restaurant was crowded, but intimate. The dining room felt private, even though every table near them was occupied.

The waiter brought their drinks and took their order.

"So, you like *Lord of the Rings*?" Kat asked.

"I'm more of a *Game of Thrones* guy," he said.

Way to go dummy, you mixed up the epic fantasy characters again. Rip would be so disappointed in her. He'd begrudgingly helped her practice by quizzing her on character names, then she went and blew it by mentioning the wrong franchise. She really should have studied harder, but honestly, what were the odds that epic-fantasy-loving-blind-date-guy was going to be hot enough to make Kat wish she were into cosplay? And come on, it was epic fantasy. Each of those books had like a hundred characters.

Whatever, moving on.

"So, have you lived here long?" she asked.

"My first visit," he said. "What about you?"

His first visit? That must be a British way of saying *I just moved here*. Maybe that was why he decided to try the dating service.

"I moved here with my best friend after high school. Did the college thing, then started working full time. The usual."

He gave her an odd look but schooled his features quickly. "Your parents must be proud."

Kat wasn't so sure about that. She knew they were proud that she got a degree—although hospitality management hadn't been their pick. They hated her job. Of course, Kat had explained a hundred times how she was using the personal assistant position to get her foot in the door at CGH. Cameron Greyson Holdings had rental properties all over the world. Kat was Cameron Greyson's personal assistant. She managed his calendar, but one day hoped to be a portfolio manager.

Someone clinked their glass, bringing Kat back to the present. "Well, they wanted me to pursue a teaching degree, but I set my goals higher. There's demand in the hospitality field."

"I see," he said.

The waiter brought their food, but the nervousness of making small talk with Mr. Sexy had taken away Kat's appetite.

Kat felt like she was blowing it. She reached up to touch her ear and realized her earring was missing. She glanced around her chair but didn't see it. Maybe it had fallen out near the bar.

Ignoring the missing bauble for now, Kat asked, "What do you do for a living?"

4

BISHOP

Bishop wasn't sure if she was being serious or fucking with him. And he could have kicked himself for that stupid comment—*your parents must be so proud*. What the fuck was he thinking?

And what was with the twenty questions? Why did she want to know what he did for a living? Was she getting information for Greyson? Was that why Greyson had hired an escort to welcome Ryker to town?

Bishop decided to play along. He'd give his cover story, but nothing else. If she pushed, he'd know something was up.

"I'm a financial consultant for a major multinational holdings company. I'm not at liberty to say more than that at present," Bishop said, continuing in his hybrid British/American accent, trying to mimic Ryker's speech exactly.

"Oh, that sounds interesting," she said with a slight hesitation, as if she had no clue what he meant.

He'd been purposefully vague. She didn't ask a follow up question about his job, which he took as a good sign Greyson hadn't sent her to spy.

Bishop noticed she'd not made a dent in her meal, moving it

around instead of eating it. He was about to ask if she wanted dessert but was stopped when she asked another question.

"Do you have any pets?"

Bishop wasn't sure what to say. He had no experience with an escort, but he didn't think idle chitchat about where he lived was a normal talking point. Was she grasping at straws to find a topic of conversation? He'd half expected her to insist they check out his hotel room, not get a table. Now she wanted to know if he had any pets.

"No," Bishop said. He had no clue if Ryker had a pet, but he didn't see how getting it wrong would matter.

"I had a boxer named Bentley growing up," she said, "But no pets now. The apartment's too small and Rip claims to be allergic, which is total BS."

"Rip?"

"Sorry, my roommate."

"The one you moved here with from high school?" Bishop asked, not exactly sure why he cared.

"Yeah, but we're not together or anything," she said, her cheeks reddening as she stammered. "I mean, we have our own rooms." She trailed off, embarrassed.

Bishop had to keep reminding himself that she was a paid escort, not the girl next door. But the blush, which was enticing as hell, and the personal questions weren't meeting his expectations. This Rip guy was probably her pimp—maybe that was how she'd gotten into this line of work. *Demand in the hospitality field, indeed.*

Stop, Bish. You're working undercover as Ryker West—not trying to save a girl from her bad choices.

Bishop motioned for the waiter to bring their check.

"Rip's not my boyfriend. We tried it once, but it didn't work out," she said, then closed her eyes. "Sorry. When I get nervous, I say too much," she said, peeking out from behind her lashes.

"You're doing fine," Bishop said, trying to remember he was supposed to be Ryker West, the guy that wanted a submissive professor type, not Special Agent Scott Bishop, who preferred his women much less meek. She was also playing a part. There probably wasn't even a Rip. "How about we go dancing?" Bishop suggested.

Her eyebrows raised slightly. Was that fear or exhilaration?

"Are there dance clubs around here?" she asked.

"The Red Martini," Bishop said, remembering the club he and Drake had checked out a few months ago.

Her mouth hung open for a beat, then said, "The Red Martini? The ridiculously posh, hard to get into, always exclusive, nightclub to the stars?"

"That's the one, love," Bishop said, not really realizing it had such a notorious reputation. He should have known. Drake wouldn't have considered buying the club otherwise.

She laughed. Glancing down at her outfit, she said, "Umm…I'll never get in."

Bishop pulled out his mobile phone. "I know a guy."

If the escort was planning to report back to Greyson the details of their evening, Greyson might question how Ryker West, a financial analyst living in Europe, had connections to a posh nightclub in New York City. But it wasn't out of the realm of possibility that Ryker could have these connections. If the escort was sent by Greyson to gather intel on Ryker, taking her back to his hotel or calling it an early evening with no attempt to use the escort's services to their full extent could be interpreted in several different ways. Bishop couldn't worry about it. Greyson's interpretation of Ryker's motives based on a date with an escort wouldn't impact the chances of the op being successful.

In any case, Bishop had already decided not to compromise his own standing within the FBI by indulging in the escort Greyson provided—even though he'd like nothing more than to get to know his paid companion better. Or at least the girl she was pretending to be.

Bishop looked up. His escort—Kat, he remembered her saying

—was smiling. He'd purposefully decided not to give her his cover name.

"Unless he owns the place," she said, "we still may be out of luck."

Bishop let the corner of his mouth turn up. He didn't say anything. Ryker West didn't know Vincent, but the escort wouldn't know who owned the club anyway. It was a total fluke Bishop knew about the Red Martini.

Bishop had planned a weekend skiing trip with his girlfriend at the time, Monica. The day before they were scheduled to leave, she'd dumped him for her personal trainer—a guy that really understood her. Drake insisted Bishop accompany him on the NYC trip to scope out the club. A distraction that Bishop needed. Red Martini was similar to Inferno, Drake's Chicago club. York Enterprises, Vincent's family's conglomerate, was interested in selling the property.

Unfortunately, Drake hadn't liked the location, and the club didn't have the same feel as Inferno, so Drake decided to pass. York Enterprise's entertainment division still owned and operated Red Martini. Bishop was hoping Vincent could pull a few strings and get him in.

Pulling up Vincent's contact, he started typing.

BISHOP: V, I need VIP access into Red Martini
VINCENT: ??
BISHOP: This is B. I'm in NYC for work...YE owns it
VINCENT: Oh...let me text Reginald
BISHOP: Give him the name West
VINCENT: OK...so it is that kind of work?
BISHOP: Yep
VINCENT: Got it

Bishop was taking a small risk asking for this favor, but he knew Vincent would keep quiet about the visit. He could trust his ex-Army Ranger buddy not to blow his cover or endanger the op. Drake and Alex, the other two members of his old Army Ranger unit, already knew he was out of town for the bureau, but the name Mr. West was generic enough that they wouldn't be able to connect him to Ryker.

Bishop saw the typing bubbles next to Vincent's name.

VINCENT: You're in…someone will meet you at the door
BISHOP: 10-4
VINCENT: Stay safe
BISHOP: Always brother, thanks!
VINCENT: Later

"It's okay if we can't get in," she said.

Damn Kat was cute. Too bad she was playing a part.

The server returned with their check. Bishop signed the receipt.

"Shall we go?" Bishop asked.

5

KAT

Kat knew there was no way they were getting in. Red Martini was one of the hottest clubs in town. Everyone wanted to be seen at the club and only a select clientele made it past the gatekeepers at the front. Even if this guy knew one of the bouncers they'd never get past the concierge at the door.

Kat's look was all wrong and no amount of Mr. I'm-So-Sexy-I'd-Rock-A-Paper-Bag was going to overshadow her fresh from the corporate day job ensemble. Rip had warned her not to leave her hair up, but she hadn't wanted to show her nervousness by constantly fussing with it—a habit she'd tried, and failed, to break. If she was the least bit stressed or anxious she'd spend the whole date twisting it into a knot or pushing it back from her face. Other dates had taken this to mean she couldn't sit still and must be an adrenaline junky—maybe that was why she attracted the hell on wheels type?

He tugged her hand, encouraging her to follow, as they approached the entrance. The line to get in was halfway around the block. Everyone was dressed to the nines, as if this were a casting call for all the beautiful people.

"It'll take hours to get through that line," she said, giving him a way out.

But Mr. I'm-So-Sexy didn't head for the back of the line. He headed straight for the guys at the velvet rope.

Kat could do nothing but stick with him.

There were three men at the head of the line and two more up the slight incline to the club's entrance. Everyone was wearing black on black except one. The two by the door and the guy manning the rope looked to be bouncers in custom fit black polo shirts with the bar's logo. The second man at the front wore a jacket, but no tie, and held a tablet, the modern-day clipboard of VIP names, she supposed. The third guy, the one not dressed like the others, checked his watch and tugged at his tie. He looked out of place in his tailored suit.

Mr. Sexy nodded to the man in the tie.

"Mr. West?" Tie Guy asked.

"Yes."

Mr. Sexy had a real name. She'd been having fun with her creative pseudonyms and had forgotten he'd never told her his name. West was so much better than Gandalf-22.

Tie Guy motioned for the bouncer to let them pass. The bouncer opened the rope. A woman near the front of the line gave Kat a snooty look. Kat ignored her, sticking close to West.

"We've got everything set for you," Tie Guy said. "VIP level access to the entire club. Full comp. If you need anything, all you have to do is ask."

"Excellent," West said.

VIP access to the entire club. Who was this guy?

The two bouncers at the door, an incredibly fit black guy that looked like he didn't take shit from anyone, and an Asian pretty boy that Rip would have been tripping over himself to flirt with, opened the doors as they approached. The Asian guy winked at her, making her re-think the Rip scenario—not that Rip would have cared if the guy was straight.

West squeezed her hand, tugging her forward.

The club pulsed to the beat of the music as they stepped through the entrance. The corridor was lined with twenty's themed wall sconces and had a vintage speakeasy feel.

According to a write-up Kat had read, the modern interior was enhanced by the timeless entryway, making it one of NYC's most iconic nightclubs.

"Anything to check?" Tie Guy asked.

West looked at Kat. She shook her head. She only had her clutch purse with her and she wasn't going to hand it over.

"No," West said.

Tie Guy led them through a second set of double doors into the main club. There was a long bar down one side, with lots of seating around small tables or on cushy couches along the back wall. A packed dance floor was off to the side. The music was thumping with a beat so intense Kat could feel it in her soul.

"This place is amazing," Kat said. She smiled up at West. "Can you dance?"

He cocked one of his gorgeous eyebrows as if Kat had just laid down a challenge.

"Want to show me some of those moves, Mr. Sexy?" Kat slapped her hand over her mouth.

West's eyes widened. Kat giggled.

"Sorry, Mr. West," she said.

West frowned, then, as if he'd remembered something, he smiled.

Taking her hand, he kissed the back of it. "Don't cover your smile," he said. "I like it when you blush, Ms. Sexy."

Kat raised an eyebrow. Mr. I-Still-Can't-Believe-His-Online-Profile-Name-Is-Gandalf-22 was flirting with her.

Kat felt the same electric reaction she'd had at the bar when he'd spun her around on the barstool.

Her thoughts were interrupted when Tie Guy cleared his throat.

"Mr. West, your private booth is this way."

"Right," he said, keeping his eyes on Kat a beat longer. "Lead the way."

Kat and West followed Tie Guy around the dance floor to a glass-walled room in the back. A guy with a tablet, dressed in the same black on black club attire she'd seen outside, was waiting for them at the door to the VIP suite. Unlike the men outside, this guy wore a red tie and had a name tag that read Chris.

"Mr. West," Tie Guy said to Chris.

Chris checked his tablet, then addressed West. "Welcome to the Red Martini, Mr. West. I'm Chris, your concierge."

Tie Guy nodded to West. "Chris will get you anything you need." Handing West a business card, he added, "If you have any issues, don't hesitate to call."

West checked the card. "Will do, Peterson," West said.

Kat wondered exactly what could go wrong that West would need to call Tie-Guy-Peterson . She'd only been in a club like this once to be Rip's wingman, and never as a VIP guest.

After a handshake with West, Peterson left. Chris led them through the door and up a short flight of stairs to the mirror-enclosed VIP area of Red Martini. The intimately lit booths and the subdued VIP atmosphere was almost a letdown, until Kat sat and looked through the glass wall into the club below. It was a fishbowl of activity. The glass was see-through from behind the mirrored surface facing the club, a voyeur's dream as bodies gyrated on the dance floor. Because the VIP floor was up a half level it presented a view that covered the entire club. Kat could look down to the dancers or straight across, over their heads, to the bar area.

"This is cool," Kat said as West sat down beside her. "My name's Kat. Kat Fox. I said that, right? I just realized we never really introduced ourselves."

6

BISHOP

Bishop smiled. He thought the name Kat suited her. Fox seemed a bit much, but then he remembered she was an escort and probably had a lot of different names she used.

Chris, the VIP concierge, interrupted Bishop's thoughts. "Jackie will be your server this evening," he said. "But don't hesitate to let me know if you need *anything* else."

Bishop didn't like the way Chris leered at Kat. The bouncer at the door had winked at her. Did they know she was an escort? She'd seemed sincere about not making it into the club, but maybe that was part of the act. Maybe she was here every other night. If Chris knew Kat was an escort, then he could be trying to let Bishop know that he could get him another girl if that was what Bishop wanted. Did Kat normally tag team?

Stop. None of this speculation was healthy. He needed to stay on point. He was here as Ryker West, not Scott Bishop. The escort was here as Kat Fox, not whatever her real name was. He needed to stay focused.

Bishop glanced at Kat, who was enamored by the club and not paying attention to his conversation with Chris.

"Right, mate," Bishop said to Chris. "So—*anything?*" Bishop placed a finger on his nose and sniffed, implying he was looking for drugs not women.

Bishop was playing Ryker, but that didn't mean Ryker couldn't get information Bishop could use later in a sting.

The corner of Chris's mouth raised. He gave an almost imperceptible nod.

"Anything," Chris agreed.

Bishop gave him a quick smile. "Do you have a card?"

Chris took out a gold metallic business card, slyly handing it over to Bishop. It didn't match the style of the card Peterson had handed him, which meant it probably wasn't a club card. He must do the illegal stuff on the side.

"I'll be in touch," Bishop said, dismissing him.

Bishop would pass the info onto Madeline. The NYC office could run the guy's info and put together a sting if they found any evidence Chris was dealing drugs out of the club.

Before Chris had a chance to say anything else, an attractive girl with long dreads and a diamond stud in her nose placed two larger than normal martini glasses on the table in front of him. It was the club's signature drink. He'd seen it before when he and Drake were here, but he'd not tried it. It was a blood red cherry martini with a twist of orange and lime as a garnish.

"This looks good," Kat said.

Picking it up she downed half of it in one go.

Bishop took a tentative sip.

"Wow," Kat said, "it's like a cherry popsicle with a little sizzle of heat. Yum."

Bishop couldn't tell what was in the drink, but he knew something this sweet would also be potent as hell. He didn't drink often and his go-to drink of choice was Guinness, not froufrou sweet drinks with a kick. He put the glass down.

"I'm Jackie," the server said. "Can I get y'all anything else?"

Her twang was light but distinct and unexpected. He'd place

that drawl in Texas or Georgia. The FBI agent in him wanted to know, but Ryker West wouldn't ask those questions unless he was sizing up a mark.

"Nothing else for me, Jackie," Bishop said. "Kat, love. Some water perhaps?"

"Mr. Sexy said we could dance." Kat smiled.

Bishop watched in shock as she reached up and started plucking pins from her hair. Was she already drunk?

"We'll take two waters," Bishop said.

"I'll have another martini," Kat said, continuing to release her hair from its twist.

Bishop glanced at Jackie and shook his head, then mouthed water.

Jackie smiled, returning to the VIP bar for the drinks.

"I can't have my hair up if we plan to dance," Kat said. "You know, West. West is an odd name. I mean it beats the hell out of Gandalf-22, right." She giggled, then snorted. "I'm sorry. I never drink. Except for that one time in college, but Rip saved me." Kat finally stopped taking pins out of her hair. She was quiet for a minute, then pushing her hair back away from her face, she started licking her lips. "That drink was really good, West."

Kat's hand reached for the glass.

"Oh, no, love. We're going to dance, remember," Bishop said.

At that moment, Jackie returned with two waters. "Anything else?"

Bishop opened the bottled water and placed it in Kat's hand. "Drink this, then we'll dance."

"Yay," Kat said, turning the bottle up to chug it like they were at a college kegger.

"Jackie, be a dear and take the martinis away," Bishop said.

Kat slammed the empty bottle down on the table. "Now we dance."

Bishop let Kat pull him from the relative quiet of the VIP section to the chaotic maelstrom that was Red Martini's dance floor. Bishop's older sisters had forced him to practice dancing with them growing up. He'd learned to swing dance before he could drive. In college he'd discovered the best way to find a hook up was to ask a girl to dance at the weekend rave.

He wasn't sure what to expect from Kat. He'd had all kinds of partners over the years, including one girl that couldn't keep a beat if her life depended on it. Would Kat be a grinder, into ballroom, or a slow dancer no matter the song?

Spinning onto the dance floor Kat's arms rose above her head. She swayed to the beat like an ethereal angel born to dance. Her eyes were alight with mischief as her fingers beckoned him forward.

Kat enveloped him with her passionate embrace as he moved to the beat, swaying in time with her hips, their bodies flowing as one. Her playfulness quickly turned to a slow deliberate roll as she slid in a sensual grind down his body as if they were having a private moment, not dancing in a mob of people.

If she kept this up for long Bishop might have to excuse himself to find a restroom. She was so fucking sexy with her wild hair cascading down her back in waves. Her body gliding in a fluid cadence with the grace of a ballerina.

God, he wished this girl was real, and he'd met her at this club as Scott Bishop, not brought her here as Ryker West's escort.

Bishop groaned as she turned away from him. Taking his hands, she placed them on her hips, using the beat to control the slow, languid stretch of her shoulder and hip as she brushed against him.

"I wish you were mine," he whispered, not expecting her to hear him.

Kat moved his hands up to her breasts. Reflexively, he squeezed.

"I can be tonight," she said.

His hands froze. This wasn't the girl next door. This was a paid companion. He could have her any night.

She twisted in his arms, facing him. Her eyes were sober now, no trace of the toxic martini in sight.

"I mean," she said, unsure of herself. "I don't know what I mean. This is my first time using the service, and you are so not what I expected." Quietly, she added, "And Rip would kill me, but..."

Bishop pulled Kat close, keeping the beat as they swayed to their own music as the frenzied crush of dancers gyrated around them.

Was she serious? Was this her first gig? Was Rip her pimp, as he'd first thought? Had she been coerced into doing this or was she playing him? He didn't believe she was playing him. There was no reason, unless she was angling to get something more permanent, but he hadn't hired her, Greyson had. She would have no reason to assume there would be a second date—a chance to propose a long-term gig as his mistress. No, she wasn't a seasoned escort. This was a new experience for her.

"I like the way you dance," she said, looking up into his eyes. "You've got moves, Mr. Sexy."

Bishop smiled. "You've had a lesson or two yourself, beautiful."

Kat rolled her hips against him. "I'm sure there's a thing or two you can still teach me."

"You're not playing fair."

"Never said I would," she purred.

KAT

The rhythm pulsed through her, causing her body to sway and grind with the heat of the moment. She was being reckless, but she didn't care. It had been years—okay, months—since she'd had a decent offer and Mr. Sexy-I've-Got-All-The-Dance-Moves West was such a hottie. He'd even saved her from that totally dangerous martini that had gone straight to her head.

And he knew how to dance.

Kat wanted to grab hold and pull his lips down to hers. She wanted to taste him as he devoured her. His strong jaw and beautiful gray-blue eyes made her want to melt into his arms and surrender.

One night of fun, that was all she wanted. They'd use protection. Everything would be okay.

Just the thought of worshiping his sexy body made Kat's legs weak and filled her stomach with butterflies. She blew out a frustrated breath and tried to ignore the raging sensations between her thighs as they continued to grind on one another.

His hand caressed her face. She tilted her chin up and leaned in. *Yes, kiss me.*

West pressed his lips to hers. A slow, sensual kiss at first. She opened her mouth, letting him deepen the moment as she silently begged for more.

The rational side of her knew she should step away. She never hooked up with guys on a first date. Of course, her fear of all things dangerous usually meant they never got to the third date—a milestone in casual dating, where you'd put up or shut up, as Rip would say. But Kat was tired of not taking the next step. She had to take a risk at some point in her life, or she was going to regret more than Rip's preference for guys. She wouldn't blame Rip. She was a big girl. She knew what happened to them wasn't her fault, had nothing to do with her sex appeal, and in the grand scheme of things meant nothing in the long run. But Rip was the guy she thought she'd marry and for a while she'd convinced herself that it might still happen.

That false hope was holding her back. This one-night stand with Mr. Sexy could flip that switch of doubt for good and give her back the confidence she needed to find her Mr. Right.

It wasn't like this guy was a complete unknown. He'd filled out the dating profile and had the background check necessary to become a member of NYC Blind Date. They had his real name, phone number, home address, and driver's license on file. For New York City, he couldn't be a safer choice. This really should tick all her boxes in that department.

She wasn't going to apologize for wanting a normal sex life. She wanted this guy for one night of no strings attached sex, and God willing, she was going to get it. She could go back to being safe Kat tomorrow.

Kat melted into his embrace, returning his kisses with equal heat. The sex starved girl who lost her virginity to her gay best friend wanted Mr. Sexy to kiss her like this all night.

When he finally pulled back, Kat might have whimpered. West chuckled. The cocky bastard knew exactly how awesome his kisses were.

"Breathe," he said, tapping her nose.

Kat blinked. Closing her mouth, she composed herself.

A new song started, *I'm Yours Tonight* by The Academy Is...

"They're playing our song," Kat said. "So how about that private dance?"

West's eyes widened. "You're dangerous...you make me want to break all my rules."

"What's stopping you?" Kat said, her heart wanting to beat right out of her chest, but she refused to back down.

West was clearly still on the fence. Damn him and his ethical dating practices. Then she remembered that she wasn't fighting fair.

"I have a PhD in exotic pole dancing," she said. Okay, so it was only one class at the local YMCA, but he didn't need to know that. Kat rolled her hips into him again. "I'd hate for you to miss out on the show."

West grabbed the back of her head, pulling her face to his. "You're bad for me, beautiful."

"I hear a but..." she breathed out before biting her lower lip.

The corner of his mouth raised in a wickedly sexy smile. "But...Tonight. You're. Mine."

8

BISHOP

Bishop couldn't believe he was doing this, but Ryker West would have had no qualms about sleeping with the escort. For some reason that bothered him. He didn't want Ryker anywhere near his girl. Whoa. Not his girl. But, damn, she played innocent like this really was her first time working as a paid companion.

He should shut this down, but he knew he wouldn't. It wouldn't hurt the case. The girl wasn't part of the operation. She was a bystander and technically hired as an escort only, with no guarantee of sex. As long as he didn't ask her to describe what she was willing to do for her fee, he had nothing to prosecute. And the FBI wouldn't go after such a small fish for a misdemeanor unless that person could roll over on the bigger fish. And there was no way Kat was connected.

They were coming up on the hotel now.

She slowed. "You're staying at the Greyson?"

"Just for a few days, love," Bishop said, taking her arm and guiding her through the door.

"Oh, cool. It's one of the premier hotels in town. A good choice."

Bishop nodded to the manager but didn't stop at the desk. He led Kat to the executive suite elevators, tapping his key card for access.

"Have you ever stayed here?" Bishop asked, hoping the answer was no.

"Just once, for an interview," she said.

Bishop had to stop himself from reacting. He'd known she wasn't...fuck, he wanted to slam her pimp into the wall a few dozen times. Her "roommate", Rip—what a fucking stupid name—had clearly backed her into a corner. Why else would she be working as a paid companion?

He composed himself as they stepped off the elevator on the top floor. If she showed any hesitation he'd stop, but Bishop hadn't initiated this step. She'd almost gotten him off with her dancing at the club. She'd wanted more.

"Are you're sure you want to do this?" Bishop asked.

Looking into his eyes, she smiled. "You've already agreed," she said.

"That I have."

Bishop opened the door to the suite and led her inside.

The door to the four-room apartment opened to a foyer. A large vase of flowers had been delivered while he was away. Compliments of the hotel, he assumed. Kat walked through to the living room, which had a large floor to ceiling window overlooking the city.

"This is a great room," she said. "The skyline is incredible from up here."

"Can I get you a drink?"

She tucked a loose strand of hair behind her ear.

"Water," she said. "No more cherry bomb martinis for me."

He smiled as she surveyed the room.

"Safe sex," she blurted out. "Do you have any condoms?" Almost to herself, she said, "I've probably got one." Fumbling with her clutch, she finally popped the latch, only to have the tiny purse slip from her hands and tip its contents onto the floor. "Holy fuck," she said, kneeling to quickly scoop up what looked like half a dozen condoms.

Bishop tried not to laugh. "Safety first," he said.

Before she could get them tucked back into her bag, he plucked one of the gold coins off the carpet.

"We'll start with this one," he said, with a wink.

She laughed. "Good choice. A real winner."

Bishop lifted her up from the floor. Taking her clutch away, he placed it on the bar. He pressed a button on the entertainment console. Soft music started to play throughout the room.

"I think you promised me a dance," he said, pulling her closer.

9

KAT

What was she doing? *About to have sex with Mr. Sexy,* she told herself as they swayed to the soulful sounds of soft jazz.

Kat was going to kill Rip. He'd put those damn condoms in her bag on purpose. She'd been mortified when they spilled out. Luckily, West laughed it off. And now they were dancing. She loved the feel of his strong arms around her as they moved with the music.

She couldn't believe she was here with him on the top floor of the Greyson, the pinnacle of CGH's top properties. She'd almost balked when it became clear he was taking her to a hotel—although after she'd had a half second to think about it, she realized it was probably safer. Of course, the safest thing to do was not sleep with a guy the first night you met him—but that ship had sailed. Tonight, Kat was the antithesis of her normal self.

Anyway, he said it was only for a few days, which meant her guess was right, he'd just moved here. And this was for one night only, right? She didn't need to know where he lived. She wasn't starting a new relationship, just a quick hook-up before she got back out there. This was the push she needed to finally move forward and dive head first into the crazy world known as the New York City dating scene. She could do this.

"Whoa," she said, as West dipped her, bringing her back to the here and now. "You've really got all the moves. Where did you learn to dance?"

West laughed. "My sisters taught me. According to them it was my fault for being so tall at twelve."

He spun her around, making her laugh.

"Well, I, for one, am glad they did."

He slowed down, raising his hand to her face, and cupped her chin. Slowly, he leaned in to kiss her. His warm lips were soft as they tenderly ravished her mouth.

West maneuvered Kat over to the window, slowly turning her to face the epic view of Manhattan at her feet. Pushing aside her hair, he grasped the zipper of her dress and pulled. He kissed the back of her neck, sending goosebumps rushing over her arms. With a soft caress, he pulled the dress off her shoulders, letting it drop to a puddle around her feet.

Thank God Kat had remembered to wear matching underwear. To feel sexy for her date, she'd picked a black lace thong and demi cup bra set she hadn't yet found a reason to wear.

"Nice," he said, turning her to face him.

"You going to stand there gawking—"

His lips were on hers before she could get the words out. She was pressed against the glass, his hands everywhere as he smothered her in kisses. She moaned as he squeezed her breast. With focused effort she started pawing at his clothes. She wanted him just as naked as she was.

Pausing a half second, he pushed her hands away and started unbuckling his pants and removing his shirt.

"The bed," he said.

"Right here," she breathed out, not wanting to lose the moment.

He smiled, then relentlessly went back to kissing her. The

sensual way he moved up and down her body was its own kind of dance. She savored and teased with her mouth, giving back all that she got.

Mr. Sexy had her flying and cresting and begging so hard she wasn't sure she'd be able to walk the next day. She lost count of how many times he had her screaming his name. His hands and mouth were all over her, sucking and biting and making her want more.

They were on condom number three by the time they made it to the bedroom.

She gasped for breath as he grabbed her wrists and lifted them above her head. He was a machine, Mr. Hot-Sexy-Unlimited-Stamina-Rollercoaster-Of-Sex-West. His other hand lightly caressed her breast, which was sore from the constant attention.

Kat was lost in the bliss of the moment as he dropped soft kisses down her neck, barely able to keep her eyes open. She needed to get up and go home, not go another round with Mr. Sexy.

He chuckled, then released her hands and dropped down over her. Kat was caged under his massively sexy body. He gave her a peck on the lips.

"I think someone is worn out," he whispered, just as she closed her eyes and let the darkness take her.

10

JAYDA

Jayda's phone buzzed. It was Evgeni.

"Answer call," Jayda said, which prompted her Bluetooth headset to activate. "What is it? I'm busy."

Jayda wasn't usually so terse with the man who had saved her life, but she was currently dragging two hundred pounds of dead weight across the dirty floor of a warehouse in New Jersey. She didn't have time to chit-chat.

"Nothing important, just an update on Sasha. He is safe," Evgeni said.

"Good," Jayda said, grunting as she heaved West into position. "One less atrocity Ana can inflict on the world."

Evgeni laughed. "My dear, your words and actions are not always in sync. Might you be the affliction Ana has released on the world? Or am I wrong and you aren't moving a dead body."

Jayda had lived and died by the sword since she was fourteen, when both of her parents were killed in a car bomb outside of a Moscow disco. She'd had no options at the time but to live on the streets. Her mother's family had disowned her the day she married Jayda's father—a man they considered to be of a lower social rank. Jayda had no extended family, but she had other skills.

By fifteen she'd fought her way out of the Krushcheby slums only to be ensnared by a ruthless madam. Evgeni had dealings with the madam, which Jayda leveraged to escape the hell that was the Jade Dragon brothel. She'd worked her way up to the accountant position, then purposefully did not pay the monthly tithe, knowing Evgeni would be sent to collect.

Jayda made her first kill the day he arrived. It had been messy, but she regretted nothing. Seeing the look on Evgeni's face when he found her standing over the bloody body of Madam Cho with her knife still dripping with blood was priceless. She'd initially planned to offer him money to take her away from the brothel, only to escape him once they were back in Moscow. But Evgeni saw something in her. He wasn't interested in sex—he wanted to train her to kill people for money. A profession she'd never considered, but thought she might like.

He asked what her name was. Little Kira was dead—two years of hell since her parents died had changed her. She would be the Jade Dragon from now on. Evgeni smiled and said he'd call her Jayda.

"My sweet," Jayda said, leaving the body to retrieve the gas can. "You are the one that released me on the world, or have you forgotten?"

"You were my best protégé," Evgeni confirmed.

"I thought I was your only protégé."

"That, too. Now, what are you doing for Ana Ivanov?"

Jayda lugged the heavy gas can over to the body. "It is no one important," she said, as she doused the body with gasoline. "Someone she suspects is tied to Nikolai, but he doesn't look all that connected to me."

"What is his name?" Evgeni asked.

"Ryker West."

Evgeni let out a long whistle. "He must have been a hard kill."

She'd drugged him as soon as they left the bar. He'd barely made it to her car before he passed out. From then on it was business as usual. She put two bullets in his head, one in his heart. Now she was burning the body. Nothing hard about it. Why was that?

"Hard in what way? Did you know West?" Jayda asked.

"I know of him. He is one of Vasili Volkov's men."

Fuck—that didn't make sense. Volkov's men were known for their strength. She shouldn't have been able to drug him so easily. At the very least he should have fought back when he realized he was going down. He'd done none of that.

She thought back to how they'd met. She'd glanced at West's picture before the op. She was looking for a man with dark blond hair and a beard. The man she met had a beard. No other man in the bar had a beard. Surely that hadn't been her only sign. She didn't often misread a situation. Bending over, she turned his face toward her and snapped a picture. Was this not Ryker West? Patting down his pockets, she looked for a wallet. Jayda almost puked when she pulled it out.

Before she even looked at his ID she knew this wasn't Ryker West. A professional underworld operative working for Volkov wouldn't carry around a green velcro wallet with a wizard patch on the outside.

Fuck me.

Jayda opened the wallet. The ID was that of Ethan Smith. Ethan fucking Smith wasn't Ryker West.

Jayda took out the ID and shoved his wallet back in his back pocket. Now that she knew he wasn't West she noticed other things. His suit wasn't well fitted, or expensive enough for a man with such impressive credentials. How had she been so sloppy.

It was the girl. The one that bumped into her at the restaurant. The one that was wearing her dress. Jayda may have been playing a part, but she still liked to stand out. The other woman had annoyed her, forced her off her game. She'd been distracted by the imitation and didn't want her interfering with the op.

Smith had seemed to expect her, which probably meant he'd

been waiting for the other girl—Jayda's double. But how did he not know what his date looked like? It wasn't like they were identical to anyone that knew either of them. Evgeni would have never mistaken the poser for Jayda. Maybe the date was arranged? A mutual friend? Fuck, that meant Smith would be missed immediately.

"You are being quiet. What is wrong?" Evgeni asked.

"Nothing. Everything is fine. I may be able to handle the Ana situation sooner than I thought. I will let you know once it is complete. Goodbye."

Jayda clicked off her earpiece. She had to move quickly. She could salvage the situation as long as no one identified Smith before she could complete her other tasks.

Jayda flipped over to her texting app. She clicked on Ana's number.

JAYDA: The job is complete. Prompt payment is expected

Jayda took another photo of Smith, this time from an angle that would not make it obvious this wasn't West. She sent that image to Ana as confirmation of the kill.

This wasn't the way Jayda worked, but she could salvage this by killing all relevant parties. It had been her plan all along—the mix up just meant she had to take care of things quicker than she'd planned. And now she needed to remove any evidence that she had been at Byron's Bistro. Smith would eventually be identified and his footsteps retraced. She couldn't allow those clues to lead to her.

Drizzling the remaining gas toward the warehouse exit, Jayda prayed for luck.

KAT

Kat woke up cocooned in strong arms.

Why am I in Rip's bed?

Cracking her eyes open, she shifted to get a better look at the room. Was that gold wallpaper and an antique arm chair? Where was she?

Grabbing her head as the pain of a headache throbbed against her skull, she started remembering the night before. This wasn't Rip's bed. And the guy in bed with her wasn't her BFF.

The arms around her tightened. The still sleepy voice muttered, "Beautiful."

What the fuck?

Had she been drinking last night? Who was this guy? *Think, Kat, think.*

The restaurant—the blind date—the nightclub—oh, fuck—the one-night stand with Mr. Sexy.

Everything about the night before came rushing back to her, including her marathon sexcapades with Mr. West. The same guy she was in bed with now. The super-hot, non-gay, fabulous dancer. And she was naked.

Naked. Fuck.

Okay, this wasn't the end of the world. She just needed to slide out of bed, find her clothes, and strut her happy walk-of-shame-ass right out the front door. She was an adult and it was her right to sleep over anywhere she damn well pleased. Now, if she could just scooch out of bed before he fully woke up—that would be awesome.

Glancing at the nightstand, she saw that it was a little before eight. Why hadn't Rip called? Where was her phone?

"What are you thinking about?" Mr. Sexy asked, ruining Kat's plan to leave before he woke up.

He nuzzled her neck, kissing up the side and taking a playful nip at her earlobe, reminding her just how good this guy was at making love.

"Nothing," she lied, not really wanting to dissect her crazy high maintenance overthinking tendencies.

He chuckled. "I know, it wasn't supposed to be a sleepover, but you conked out on me, love."

Who wouldn't, she thought. He was like a sexpert with stamina. The things he did with his tongue were probably illegal in most of the southern states. If Kat were still Catholic, she'd need the confessional.

Okay, stop stressing. Everyone had a good time. He'd used protection. She just needed to put this in the "oh, what a night" column and never speak of it again. To anyone. Ever.

She cleared her throat, but he spoke first.

"Don't worry, I'll pay extra. You were worth it." Rolling away from her, he smacked Kat's ass as he jumped out of the bed.

Kat lay there stunned as he headed toward the bathroom. Was he joking?

He didn't look back.

Holy fuck, he thought I was a hooker?

She was still laying there with her mouth hanging open as she heard him start to pee.

That sound, and the faint trill of an incoming text message knocked her out of her stupor.

Another chirp sounded. She had to get the hell out of this place.

Throwing off the sheet she got to her feet. Her head was spinning and her body was sore, but she ignored it. Quickly she found her clothes and shimmied into her dress. Her bra was nowhere to be found. She grabbed his shirt and threw it on over the rumpled dress. With shoes, phone, and clutch in hand she was out the door before he'd flushed the toilet.

As Kat headed down the hall in the most epic walk of shame ensemble ever, the elevator dinged. She ducked into the vending room and waited. Within seconds a tall, take-no-shit blonde strode by. She was talking on the phone.

Kat overheard her say, "Bishop, answer your fucking phone. I'm almost there. You better be up."

After the woman passed, Kat quietly slipped out of the little alcove and made it to the elevator. She pressed the down arrow. The door opened immediately. Good, she'd caught it before it was called away.

Kat slapped the button for the lobby and prayed no one else would get on as she descended.

Finger combing her hair and rolling up the shirt's sleeves, she did her best to make herself presentable. She knew she wasn't fooling anyone. One look and they'd probably think she was a hooker, too.

The most epic one-night stand dating fail ever.

She wiped away a tear as she reached the lobby. She had to keep her shit together and get home. She could cry then.

As the elevator popped open, Kat sprang from the box as if the hounds of hell followed her. She dashed through the posh entrance and jumped into a waiting taxi, totally pissing off an Asian businessman who had been about to enter.

"Twenty extra tip if you get me the hell out of here right now," she said to the cabby.

He paused a half second, then turned on the meter and pulled into traffic.

Kat didn't look back to see if the Asian guy was cursing her or not. She just wanted to pretend none of this had ever happened. She wanted to curl up in her own bed and forget she'd just slept with a guy that thought she sold herself for a living.

"You okay, miss?" the cabby with a distinctly island accent asked.

Kat knew she looked disheveled, as she wiped away more tears. "Yeah, just a rough night."

"You want to go—"

"Home," she said, before he could suggest anything like the police.

Kat gave him the address, then sunk back into the seat. She was ready to put this whole incident in her rear view. Nothing Mr. I-Pay-For-My-Sex had done was unwanted—aside from thinking he'd hired her as a hooker.

She chuckled.

"You crazy, miss?" the cabby asked.

"Probably," she said.

Thinking back to the restaurant, Kat remembered her doppelgänger and laughed again. Had he been there for her? Or were there three women walking around in a blue dress last night? He had said she was exactly what he'd ordered. Fuck, she was an idiot.

Oh, no, what had happened to her date? Maybe Gandalf-22 got lucky.

Kat opened the messenger app on her phone. She texted Rip.

KAT: PLEASE go get coffee from Local Joe's—I'll owe
    you big!
RIP: UGH, I'm still in the bed, you go

RIP: When did you get in?
RIP: You didn't get in did you, you dog
RIP: I want to know everything
KAT: Please just get the coffee
RIP: Are you sending me away so your walk of shame isn't recorded?
KAT: You wouldn't…or I'll share the pictures of you drunk kissing your cousin Michael
RIP: That's cold Kit Kat
KAT: Just get the damn coffee. Please.
RIP: Only if you promise to tell me everything—like how you got into the Red Martini…

Fuck, how did he find out about that? The guy at the door, the one that winked. She knew he looked familiar. That was one of Rip's hook-ups. It had to be.

Kat texted back.

KAT: Coffee—then I'll explain
RIP: Fine. Leaving now

It would take Rip at least twenty minutes to complete the coffee run. Five to get there and back and ten minutes to flirt with the barista. She was in total denial mode by the time she made it to the apartment. She had ten minutes to burn her clothes, shower, and get presentable. For the first time ever, she wished she lived alone.

12

BISHOP

"So, Ms. Sexy—" Bishop said as he left the bathroom.

Kat wasn't in the bed where he'd left her. He grabbed his phone from the nightstand and headed into the living room. Kat wasn't there either. He glanced around. Her clothes were gone. Why had she left?

His phone chirped. He looked down. One missed call and a text.

"Fuck," he cursed. Mad Max was on her way up.

He quickly texted Madeline back.

BISHOP: Don't come up

Just as he hit send, he heard a single knock and the door lock click. *Fuck. Does Madeline have her own key?*

"Ryker, darling, are you decent?" Madeline called out from the foyer.

A second voice, male, said, "Room service."

It was the breakfast order he'd placed yesterday.

Ignoring Madeline, Bishop directed the server to leave the

food tray on the bar. Bishop signed the check and waited for the attendant to leave before addressing Madeline.

"What the fuck are you doing here, Max?" Bishop asked.

Madeline laughed as she entered the living room. She was dressed in an expensively tailored red business suit with a slit too high for corporate America. Her blonde hair was perfectly styled in a tight chignon to emphasize her bulletproof, take no prisoners persona. She was two years older than Bishop, but even at thirty-five she had the body of a woman who knew how to take care of herself.

"I knew you'd be alone," she cooed. "No three-grand hooker stays the night for anything less than ten-k."

Bishop just stared at her. Madeline had no clue what Kat was paid by Greyson, but that was beside the point. He wasn't going to confirm or deny her suspicions. Kat had ducked out without a goodbye. He sure as shit wasn't letting Madeline know that detail.

As Madeline sauntered through to the couch, a wry smile crossed her face. She bent to swipe something off the floor. Chuckling, she held out her index finger. It was Kat's bra.

Bishop didn't say anything, but his facial expression must have switched from annoyed to fuck you.

"Quit looking at me like that," she said. "I requisitioned the cash, remember. I'm glad you put it to good use."

Madeline glanced around the room as if she needed more proof he'd slept with the escort.

Ignoring her, Bishop stepped over to the bar and poured himself an orange juice.

"No juice for me, thanks," she said.

"You aren't staying."

Madeline pouted. "Scott, you used to be so much fun. What happened?"

"What do you want, Max? Shouldn't you be interrogating the real Ryker West?" Bishop asked.

"You know there's nothing there. We just needed him out of the way so you could bait Greyson."

Bishop raised an eyebrow. Was she serious, or just not willing to share any information? He'd originally come to the city to do some simple surveillance. Madeline's op was charged with getting more intel on Greyson for a future sting operation. Her team consisted of himself and Jerry Osborn, a newbie agent she was mentoring.

Bishop hadn't hit it off with Jerry. He was too green and he hero worshiped Madeline as if she somehow wrote the rule book on how to be a successful agent. The op then transformed into a sting, so obviously Bishop expected Madeline to interrogate Ryker. If for no other reason than to get corroborating evidence that Ryker specifically came to New York to launder money.

"What if West is more than simply a new client? I'm only going to get one shot at this. If Greyson doesn't take the bait, we've got nothing."

Madeline rolled her eyes.

"Is West being held at headquarters? Is someone else doing the interrogation? You didn't leave Jerry in charge, did you?"

"Scott, you need to get over Jerry's role in the op. You and he are at the same level, remember?"

Fuck, no, he wasn't. The kid had been on the job for three weeks. This was his very first assignment. Madeline was Jerry's mentor, for fuck's sake. Bishop was a seasoned agent that normally ran his own ops. He was more qualified than Madeline.

But he didn't say any of that. It wouldn't help his case or get Madeline to change. "What's our next move if this thing with Greyson doesn't work?" Bishop asked.

"Quit worrying about my part. I have things under control. Jerry is watching Ryker. You just need to focus on flipping Greyson."

"Watching Ryker? Where, at FBI headquarters?" Bishop asked.

"I've got Ryker at a safe location. Don't worry about that, it's covered," she said.

"Is Reece aware of your strategy?"

Madeline looked offended. "The ADIC has given me the authority to run this op as I see fit. You're the one with questionable case handling skills, not me."

Bishop's jaw tightened. He had to avoid these types of conflicts. Madeline saw any challenge to her handling of the op as some sort of attempt to make her look bad.

Bishop's meeting with Greyson was a standard meet and greet. If Greyson didn't fall for their ruse and offer to launder Volkov's money, there wasn't a different play. Regardless of what Madeline's grand plan was, West couldn't be held indefinitely. Bishop didn't know enough about the real Ryker West's business affairs to bluff for a second meeting. The intel had been sketchy at best and barely enough to work with for one meeting. If Madeline blew the opportunity to interrogate West, that was on her. It wasn't the way he'd have run this op, but Bishop was in no position to drive her down a different path. Especially if Reece was letting her run with this lead. He didn't have to like it, but he couldn't do a damn thing about it. He had to stay the course and attempt to get Greyson to incriminate himself. Bishop had no other options, but this was the last time he'd ever agree to be part of a Mad Max op.

"You're right. It's your case, Max. If Greyson doesn't take the bait, oh well, I guess we'll just go back to surveillance," Bishop said sarcastically.

"Now, Scott, don't be like that. Greyson is so dirty anyone could get him to incriminate himself," she cooed.

Bishop didn't respond to her dig.

Madeline opened the top button of her blouse, exposing her cleavage. "I thought we could reminisce about old times."

Bishop barked out a laugh. "No."

"Are you sure?" she purred.

Bishop rolled his eyes. He'd had enough of her bullshit.

"I agreed not to discuss our past with your ADIC. If you somehow think that gives you leverage over me, think again. I discussed it with my ADIC. He and I agreed it wouldn't be an issue. You need to button up your top and get back to doing your job. And Madeline, if you know what's good for you, you'll interrogate West. If for no other reason than to cover your own ass. You had the man arrested. You'll need something to show for the effort."

Madeline stood, straightening her skirt. Her lips were pursed. Clearly, she didn't like being told no. Bishop didn't give a fuck.

Heading to the door, she said, "Answer your damn phone next time and I won't have to make a house call."

13

KAT

Kat was camped out on the sofa waiting for Rip to return with her coffee. The apartment wasn't big, but they each had a bedroom and shower to call their own. The apartment felt cluttered today, but even on its best day the tragically eclectic boho chic collection of furniture wasn't going to win any style awards. The couch was the nicest piece. The too-heavy-to-move behemoth had been inherited from the previous tenant.

"Kit Kat," Rip called as he opened the door. "Your knight in shining armor has arrived with the elixir of life."

Kat was in her softest PJs, hugging her knees to her chest. Her hair was still wet from the shower as she hadn't bothered to dry it.

Rip stopped in his tracks when he spotted her.

Her eyes were red from crying, but she didn't care. She just wanted to forget about last night, but she knew that wasn't completely possible.

"Kat. What the fuck happened?" Rip said, his tone serious.

She shook her head, wiping away another tear as it fell. "Nothing—just a misunderstanding," she said, trying to blow it off.

Rip put the coffee down on the end table. Sitting beside her, he wrapped his strong arms around her.

"You don't cry. Ever," he said, kissing her on the top of the head. "So, you want to try that again?"

Kat knew Rip would want to know, and clearly she was unable to hide it from him.

"What bastard do I need to hunt down and kill?"

She gave a halfhearted laugh. If only it was that simple. "It wasn't like that. Not really."

"Okay, what was it like. Tell me. Did he hurt you?"

She shook her head. "No. He was incredible. Never been laid better." Before he could protest, she added, "This isn't about you, remember."

He kissed her on the top of the head again. "Okay, so best lay ever guy did something wrong. What was it?"

"Oh, you know. The usual," she swallowed, still not able to believe what happened. "He said he'd pay extra because I'd slept over."

Rip was speechless.

"Yeah," she said. "My thoughts exactly."

"But you were on the blind date, right? Did the guy think he'd signed up for an escort?" Rip asked. "The service was legit. I checked it out."

Kat hadn't known Rip had done that, but she wasn't surprised. He was always looking out for her.

"Remember my doppelgänger at Byron's Bistro?" she asked. "I think maybe she was supposed to be Mr. Sexy's escort."

"No fucking way. That means she got your date."

Kat shrugged. "Maybe. I don't know."

Rip tightened his arms around her. "You said it only got weird when he offered to pay you? What did you say to him?"

"Nothing. I snuck out while he was in the can."

Rip chuckled. "Fucking hell. That was probably the best plan."

"What would you have done?" Kat asked.

"Taken the money, for one."

Kat looked at him. "No, you wouldn't have."

"Fuck yeah. If he thought he was paying for it, that meant he got exactly what he wanted."

Kat settled back against Rip's warm chest. "He didn't disappoint."

"That good, huh?"

"Oh, yeah. That good."

"And he took you to the Red Martini—I can't believe you went without me," Rip said.

"Who told you?" Kat asked, curious if her theory was right.

"I got a text last night from an unknown number. Turned out to be Riku, that guy I banged last week at Gina's party."

"You banged him last week and his number is already out of your phone?"

"He was a clinger. Had to let him go," Rip said, with absolutely no remorse.

"Okay, good to know."

"Then what? You didn't go to his apartment, did you?"

Kat shook her head. "No, he was staying at the Greyson. I thought he'd just moved to town. Clearly my investigative skills are lacking. He had the sexist voice though—kind of British, but American at the same time."

"Good, that means he's here on business and will be gone soon enough. No risk of running into him again."

Actually, she wished Mr. Sexy was really Gandalf-22 and she could set up another date, but that wasn't possible and hadn't been her original plan anyway. He was supposed to be the one-night stand guy that got her back on the dating scene—not an out of town businessman who paid for sex.

"Hand me my clutch," Kat said, pointing at the side table behind Rip. She wanted to remove the condoms before she forgot about them. "And thanks a lot for all the condoms, jerk. I totally upended my damn purse, and they all fell out."

Rip laughed. "Well, he already thought you were a hooker, babe, so I'm not sure it shocked him."

Kat hadn't even considered that until Rip mentioned it. "Awesome," she said sarcastically.

Rip handed Kat her bag. "I want the ones back you didn't use. You should keep one, though, just in case."

Kat rolled her eyes. Popping open her clutch, she gasped. Pushing off the couch, she dropped the purse.

"No. No fucking way," she said.

Rip, confused, grabbed the clutch. Looking inside, he whistled. "Fucking hell, babe," he said as he removed the wad of cash from her bag. Counting it, he said, "Three-K. You're apparently worth three thousand dollars a night, babe."

"I'm not touching that money. I want you to get rid of it."

"Ummm...not sure what you expect me to do with it. Rent's due."

Kat just scowled at him.

"Okay, okay. I'll find a charity you can give it to."

Kat stomped off toward her bedroom.

"Ohmygod, you used three condoms?" Rip called after her. "Holy fuck, is he bi?"

Mortified, Kat shut her bedroom door. She wanted to curl up in her bed and forget she'd ever met Mr. Sexy.

14

BISHOP

Bishop couldn't stop thinking about Kat. It was stupid. She was an escort that got paid. He'd originally considered not paying her the tip money, which would have meant the agency couldn't use that payment as leverage to force her to testify against Greyson, but how would Bishop explain that behavior to the bureau. He'd slipped the money in her clutch after she'd fallen asleep, then she'd left before he had a chance to rethink the plan. He hadn't expected her to sneak out while he was in the bathroom, but she had no obligation to sleep over or hang around the next morning—so he needed to get over it.

Bishop considered asking Greyson for the contact information for Kat's agency, but what exactly did he think he'd do with it? FBI Special Agent Scott Bishop certainly couldn't use it. For now he had to forget about her. After this mission was over he'd try to track her down himself. Maybe Alex—no way, he wasn't going to be responsible for getting his friend in more trouble. Alex couldn't run anymore illegal searches. He'd gotten off easy with the stunt he pulled helping Drake. Alex had to stay clear of anything that was even remotely illegal, or he'd wind up in jail.

Bishop checked the time. He had an hour and a half before he was scheduled to meet Greyson at the Four Seasons for brunch. Taking out his phone, he brought up the last text from Vincent.

> BISHOP: V, Red Martini may have a problem with one of the concierges—Chris made it very clear he could get Mr. West anything he needed. I've emailed NYC bureau office about it as well

Within seconds he saw typing bubbles appear on the screen. Bishop clicked over to Uber. He typed in the restaurant's address and selected a premium vehicle. Driver ETA was five minutes.

His phone dinged and he switched back to Vincent's text.

> VINCENT: 10-4. I'll let Reginald know
> VINCENT: How was the club?
> BISHOP: Nice, didn't stay long
> VINCENT: Alex just told me to tell you to text him
> BISHOP: Are we in high school?
> VINCENT: No jackass, we're playing WOW and he mentioned it
> BISHOP: 10-4

Bishop switched over to text Alex, just as the Uber app pinged him indicating the car was close. He left the hotel room and headed downstairs.

> BISHOP: A, what's up, too busy to copy my number from V?
> ALEX: LOL, no, but I know you're busy. Ana was spotted in NYC
> BISHOP: How do you know that?
> ALEX: Overheard Meghan talking to Tyson

Meghan Malone was Alex's FBI supervisor while he was

working off his deferred community service for the bureau instead of jail, but Bishop hadn't realized that Alex would be spending enough time with the agent to overhear that type of intel. At least, Bishop hoped Alex was collaborating with her and not bugging the FBI office where they worked.

The elevator dinged, opening onto the lobby. His phone chirped at the same time, letting him know his car had arrived. Bishop exited the hotel. A new luxury town car was waiting for him at the curb. After a few pleasantries to the driver, he replied to Alex.

BISHOP: Does she know you know?

After a long pause of inactivity, Bishop asked again

BISHOP: Alex, does she know?
ALEX: 10-4, but Tyson doesn't...it was just a coincidence, I didn't try to overhear it.

Bishop wasn't sure what he should do. He had no intention of calling out his friend, Alex, for something so trivial, but Meghan should be more circumspect with her surroundings. Alex shouldn't have been able to overhear sensitive info, regardless of whether Meghan was aware or not.

He texted Alex back.

BISHOP: Don't be stupid with your access. Thanks for the heads up
ALEX: Roger that
ALEX: So I guess that means you don't want the Evgeni update?

Bishop pinched the bridge of his nose. Alex was going to get thrown in prison if he kept this crap up.

Unwilling to let the information languish, he texted.

BISHOP: What is it…and no, you aren't getting off the hook about this. I will be talking to Meghan when I get back
ALEX: Please don't, it really isn't her fault. I'll be less nosy

Bishop wasn't sure he believed that was possible, but he decided to let it go for now. He wanted the info about Evgeni and knew he couldn't get it from Tyson. Not while he was on this assignment with Madeline. Another text from Alex came in.

ALEX: Evgeni has been spotted in Detroit and they have wiretaps of him talking to a contact that goes by the name Jayda Dragon. She's a contract killer—a past with some really fucked up shit. She's worked for Ana Ivanov before too
BISHOP: Is he hiring her to take out Ana?
ALEX: Unknown. Conversation we intercepted was in code, techs are still working on it
BISHOP: Do we have a photo?
ALEX: Negative
BISHOP: Roger that, and please try to stay out of trouble. You wouldn't like prison
ALEX: 10-4

Bishop had firsthand experience. Not prison exactly, but being in a military brig on a large base wasn't far from it. He, Drake, and Vincent had spent several weeks in limbo while the higher ups sorted out the debacle that got them discharged. A mission had gone south, they almost got caught by the Ortega cartel, and Alex lost his leg.

Alex had been in lockdown at the Army Medical Center during that same time. He'd not had the same experience as the others but was discharged with everyone else after the investigation.

The connection Drake's girlfriend, Haden, had with the cartel had finally shaken some things loose. General Davis was able to connect the fucked mission with Ortega. And although Bishop and his buddies had never been charged with anything, their names were finally being cleared. The Dangerous Eight was no longer a cursed moniker. Not that it mattered. He and the guys had all moved on. Bishop enjoyed his job at the bureau. He'd just traded one way of serving his country for another, and he was okay with that. He wasn't sure the other guys felt the same, but he'd made his peace already.

Bishop's phone chirped again. It was another text from Alex.

> ALEX: Don't be pissed…last thing…Meghan said you're in the doghouse. Is that true

Bishop wasn't sure how to answer that. It was complicated. From the FBI's perspective, his friends, including Alex, had really fucked up. Their actions during the op brought into question how much intel Bishop had shared with them. That was why Bishop needed to make this temp assignment with Madeline work. He'd been willing to take the lower assignment to get him out of Chicago for a while. It gave Tyson the room he needed to wrap up the Ortega case without having Bishop underfoot. And it gave Bishop a chance to prove himself. The original assignment for surveillance would have been a better gig for laying low, but Ryker West was an opportunity they couldn't ignore. Bishop had a chance to help break this case against Greyson wide open, not just watch Greyson to gather intel for another team to act. Unless Madeline screwed things up on her end, this case could put Bishop back on track for leading the office one day. But he couldn't think about that right now. He had to focus on the assignment and do his best to convince Greyson he was Ryker West.

Bishop would get Greyson to propose a strategy to clean Volkov's money. That was his part and he had to make it work.

Looking back at his phone, he started typing.

BISHOP: I'm okay, just keep YOUR nose clean. I mean it
ALEX: Roger that

Bishop wasn't sure what to do with the Ana information. Wilson, his ADIC in Chicago, had made it very clear—he wasn't working the Ivanov/Ortega case. Tyson was the lead on that case and Bishop had been ordered to stay out of it.

"We're here," the driver said.

Bishop looked up. "We're on the wrong side of the street."

"The other way was blocked. You can cross at the light."

Bishop didn't argue with the driver. He was ten minutes early for the meeting. He had time to cross the street. After exiting the car, he made his way to the corner and waited for the light to change. As he stood there, a black Audi Q7 SUV pulled up in front of the restaurant. Bishop knew from the prep he'd done on Cameron Greyson that the Q7 was his car of choice. What he hadn't expected was to see Ana Ivanov exit the car with Greyson.

What the fuck?

The light changed. As Bishop crossed the street, he snapped several pictures of Ana and Greyson. He continued down the street alongside the Four Seasons hotel. He watched as Ana returned to the SUV and it drove away. Greyson continued into the hotel's restaurant.

Bishop pulled up the pictures. Selecting the two with the best shot of Ana and Greyson together, he emailed those to Madeline. Switching to his contacts, he called her phone.

"How may I direct your call?" Madeline answered, a standard greeting for an agent in the field.

"Max, did you get the pictures? I just emailed them," Bishop said.

"Yes, I'm looking at them now. Where are you?"

"Outside the restaurant, alongside the hotel. Ivanov left in the SUV, Greyson went into the restaurant alone."

"Did she see you? Would she know who you are?" Madeline asked.

"Negative. She's never met me and I'm not officially tied to the case in Chicago. I was in a crowd when I crossed the street. Neither she nor Greyson spotted me."

"Good. Take the meeting. Forget you spotted Ana."

"You need to notify Tyson and the ADIC in Chicago," Bishop said.

Madeline paused for a minute. Was he keeping her from something? He was about to say something, when she finally spoke.

"I'll notify Reece," she said with no urgency. "He'll handle passing on the information to the others. You stay in character. We need Greyson's confession now more than ever. If we can flip him, he'll turn on Ivanov."

"Ivanov is now the head of her family. Why would she be with Greyson? Is there something more to this case that we are missing?" Bishop asked.

"Scott—"

"Hear me out. If Ivanov is tied to Greyson to launder money for the family, that would be huge. Or could she be using the Greyson connection to set up a meeting with Volkov? What have you learned from Ryker?"

"Stick to what you know, Scott. Let me worry about the bigger picture."

Madeline disconnected the call.

"What the fuck," Bishop said, checking his screen to verify she'd hung up on him.

Bishop was about to call her back when a group text came in from Jerry.

JERRY: Found a match on West's prints from a DD case
near Chicago about a year ago. Email sent with details
MADELINE: I'm not near my computer. Bring the paper
report and return to alpha base
JERRY: Will do

Bishop switched over to his email, but there was nothing from Jerry. Bishop switched back to his chat to text back, then stopped. Bishop probably wasn't meant to get that text. Maybe Jerry accidentally selected his name when texting Madeline. Opening his contacts, he selected Jerry's name and clicked the message button, opening a new chat session.

BISHOP: Madeline wants you to forward me the
West email
JERRY: Why?
BISHOP: Until I see it I won't know
JERRY: Fine

Bishop wanted to strangle the kid. Jerry needed to get out from under Madeline or he'd never be a good agent to partner with. Bishop was on the team, for fuck's sake. Jerry had no reason to withhold information.

Bishop switched back to his email. The forwarded email was there. Bishop quickly scanned the details.

The attachment was a drunk driving report against Walter Bacon. His blood alcohol level was triple the limit, and he'd been arrested for public drunkenness in the past. The victim was Sarah Daniels. She died when Bacon ran her car off the road.

What the fuck. Sarah Daniels was his buddy Drake's old girlfriend—the one that was killed by a drunk driver months before he met Haden. How the hell was she tied to Ryker West?

Skimming the rest of the file Bishop found it. Along with

Bacon's prints, a partial thumbprint taken from Bacon's car was a match to the prints they took off West.

Ryker West was supposed to be the financial analyst to Vasili Volkov, a criminal running black market goods between Russia and the UK, so what the hell were his prints doing in Chicago ten months ago? Was he really in town to get Greyson to launder Volkov's money, or was that all a ruse? Who the fuck was Ryker West?

Bishop pulled up his chat with Alex. No. He couldn't have his buddy look into West. Especially not now, because the West situation was somehow indirectly connected to Drake because of Daniels. How the hell that was even possible, he had no idea.

Bishop put away his phone and straightened his suit. He had to complete the meeting with Greyson, then he was getting answers from Madeline.

15

JAYDA

Jayda's phone buzzed. It was a text from her FBI contact, Madeline Maxwell. Jayda didn't normally cultivate assets within the US government agencies, but Madeline had been Ana's go-to fixer for several years. After the clusterfuck that killed Ana's father and son, Ana began purging dead weight. Ana had instructed Jayda to kill Madeline, but Ana never offered to pay Jayda for the job. Jayda opted to continue communicating with Madeline instead, pretending to be Ana. Unfortunately, after a few interactions, it was clear why Ana had planned to eliminate the high-ranking agent. Madeline was fucking nuts. She'd recently become obsessed with climbing the corporate ladder, and for some reason thought Ana could help make that a reality. She'd also started using again, which made her unpredictable. Cocaine wasn't a recreational drug.

Jayda flipped over to her texting app.

FBI_FOOL: What are you doing with Cameron Greyson? My agent just spotted you with him

Jayda was confused at first, then remembered Madeline thought she was Ana. She texted back.

> JAYDA: He is a business partner. Nothing to concern you
> FBI_FOOL: I told you about my big case—you didn't mention that you knew him?!?

Fuck, that was probably another reason Ana wanted Madeline eliminated. She'd started poking into Greyson's business dealings, which was how Ana had made most of her money before her father's death left the Ivanov fortune under her control.

Jayda considered a few options to back out of the conversation, then realized what Madeline was saying. Her agent had seen Ana with Greyson. Who the fuck was her agent and why was Ana with Greyson today? Greyson was next on Jayda's hit list. Shouldn't Ana be distancing herself from the mark?

Jayda texted back. She needed more info.

> JAYDA: What agent do you have following me? I thought your investigation was around Greyson's financials

Jayda wasn't sure what Madeline and Ana had discussed, but being defensive and implying Madeline's investigation was somehow insignificant might rile her up enough to spill relevant details.

Madeline was typing, and typing, and typing. Jayda wanted to scream. Would she spit it out already. Finally, the text arrived.

> FBI_FOOL: My agent is following Greyson, not you. He has a meeting with Greyson today. This investigation is about more than what Greyson pays in taxes. This is a serious crackdown on the illegal foreign money he has pouring in from overseas. What business do you have

with him? If it's to launder money you need to sever ties. I won't be able to protect you once this goes public

This was all Jayda needed. But it sounded like Madeline didn't know Ana was the one pulling Greyson's strings. If Madeline's investigation turned up Joseph Koshy's name, Madeline would be closer to the truth of Ana's involvement, but Ana would be dead by then. Jayda just needed to ride out this storm.

Jayda's phone buzzed with another incoming text.

Fuck. The text was from Ana.

ANA: You took out the wrong man. West arrived to meet Greyson. WTF happened?

Jayda couldn't believe her luck. Of course Ana was seeing Greyson today, and of course West and Greyson had a meeting. Dammit. A text came in from Madeline, reminding Jayda of her other problem.

Jayda texted Madeline back first. She'd planned to just stop taking her calls, but now she'd have to consider killing Madeline, too, if she somehow got evidence linking Jayda Dragon to her op involving Greyson. Fucking hell.

JAYDA: No worries, our dealings are legit. Ryker West is your agent? I thought he worked for Volkov

FBI_FOOL: I can't confirm or deny, but you need to stay away from that meeting

Jayda had no control over whether or not Ana was attending the meeting. A new text from Ana popped up. It was an image. Jayda clicked the icon to enlarge.

The picture appeared to have been taken from outside the restaurant. Greyson and the man with him were too far away for a positive ID, but Jayda had seen enough images of Greyson to recognize him instantly. His hair, brown with a bold stripe of white down one side, was distinctive. The man with him was younger, early thirties, with light hair. He resembled the pictures she had of West, but this man was clean shaven. This wasn't West, it was Madeline's agent. The image also meant Ana wasn't actually at Greyson's meeting.

The agent must have seen Ana with Greyson before the meeting and reported it back to Madeline. But if this man wasn't West, where was Ryker West?

Jayda texted Madeline back.

> JAYDA: I'm not at the meeting, but neither is West. Who do you have pretending to be West? Where is the real Ryker?

Madeline didn't immediately respond. Jayda switched back to Ana's chat.

> JAYDA: That man isn't Ryker West

Jayda had no proof, but it was a story she could sell. She only needed two days, after that everyone would be dead and she could skip town before Smith's body was identified.

Ana texted back.

> ANA: Who the fuck is it?
> JAYDA: FBI agent would be my guess. Greyson is a liability. I recommend we complete our business sooner rather than later.
> ANA: Agreed. Send proof of completion on Greyson and payment will be processed immediately
> JAYDA: I'll need the payment in cash. I need to disappear for a few weeks.
> ANA: Fine. Text me when you're done and I'll arrange it.

JAYDA: Expect notification by tomorrow evening.
ANA: Don't disappoint me again

Jayda didn't respond. She'd take care of Ana, then Madeline, and anyone else she needed to kill to make it out of this shit show alive. Jayda checked the time. She had to wash her hair one more time or the pink would be a bright beacon to anyone that saw her and she needed anonymity to get rid of the video at the bistro. But to do that she had to be there before it opened, which meant she had to get moving.

16

RYKER

Ryker studied the woman that entered the room. She took the seat across from him. Her eyes were wide. She had large dilated pupils, with an edge to her demeanor that he didn't like. Was she naturally high-strung or was she on something?

She placed a mobile phone on the table between them and pressed record. She didn't immediately introduce herself, or give her rank. Ryker was tired of waiting. It was his second day in this shithole and no one had read him his rights or provided him with an attorney.

"Lawyer," Ryker said.

"You're not yet being interrogated, Mr. West. We're just chatting here," she said. "There's no need for a lawyer."

Ryker held up his manacled wrists. "I'm in custody." He rattled the chains against the metal loop securing him to the table. "I want my phone call."

Ignoring him, she continued. "Please state your name for the record."

Ryker remained silent.

"You're required by law to provide identification."

Ryker gave her a tight smile, then said, "My name is Ryker West."

"How long have you known Cameron Greyson?"

"I demand that you contact my attorney, Edward. Watson. Esquire," Ryker said with slow deliberate speech.

She ignored his request. "Let's talk about Ivanov's connection to Greyson."

She waited for Ryker's reaction. He gave her nothing.

"Perhaps we should talk about Sarah Daniels."

What. The. Fuck. How did she know about Sarah Daniels? The CIA should have buried that case with all the others. Had someone fucked up, or were they trying to burn him?

The TSA agents that had *randomly* selected him from the security line said they found a ten-year-old warrant from Texas. They had supposedly handed him off to the FBI—now this woman was bringing up Daniels. Daniels was a side project he handled for General Davis, his old Army Ranger commander, but the CIA had sanctioned the hit—so how the hell did this woman link them?

The woman slammed her hand on the desk.

Ryker looked up, his attention returning to the supposed agent in front of him.

"I'm talking to you," she said. "You need to get smart. If you want to leave this holding cell, you'll need to start cooperating."

Ryker raised an eyebrow. "Lawyer. Edward. Watson. Esquire," he said, repeating his code phrase.

If this was really the FBI, their techs should be searching that name right now and getting in contact with his CIA handler.

"We'll get to your lawyer soon," she said, dismissively. "First, I want to know what you know about Greyson's connection to Ana Ivanov."

Ana Ivanov, Nick's little sister. Interesting that they'd focus on her. Ryker wasn't aware the FBI knew of her involvement with Greyson. Did that mean they also knew about Nick? No, if the

FBI knew of the CIA's plans to take out Ana and put Nikolai Ivanov in charge of the Ivanov clan, they'd know not to interfere.

Ryker glanced at the mobile phone, which he'd initially thought was a prop. Was she not using the room's surveillance? Fucking hell. Was she rogue?

"You'll start talking, or I'll have Jerry throw you back in your cell and let you stew for a few days. I hope you like the stale water coming out of the tap, because that's all you'll get."

Ryker laughed. He'd slogged his way through dense jungle where the only water he could drink had to be purified first. Fucking stale tap water was a joke.

"What are you laughing at?" the woman yelled.

"Jerry?" Ryker asked, raising his right eyebrow. "Who the fuck are you? Tom?"

Her eyes widened, then narrowed. Her nostrils flared as she flew into a rage. "I'm FBI Special Agent Madeline Maxwell, jackass, and I'm about to be your worst nightmare."

Ryker kept a steady pace to his breathing. If he weren't handcuffed to the table, he'd have already put her in a choke hold. He'd never heard of Madeline Maxwell, but as soon as he got out of here he'd find out who the fuck she was and end her career.

"You don't scare me, sweetheart," Ryker said. "I've been questioned by harder men than you."

Calmly, as if she hadn't just lost her shit a minute ago, she said, "Was that while you were doing business for Volkov, or should I say Nikolai Ivanov?"

Ryker's lip curved up, but not for the reason she was probably assuming. Nick would get a kick out of someone thinking he was Volkov.

Nikolai Ivanov did business under his own name. Vasili Volkov was the cover Ryker had appropriated for himself when he was forced to join the CIA. He'd been using it for years, so he could play the "I'm just the help" card. Nick had figured out that Ryker was Volkov. He'd not discovered that Ryker was CIA, however, which was why Ryker was still tangled up in all this mess and not back home in Texas with this undercover gig only in his memory.

"Did you hear my question, West? Is Ivanov really Volkov? Now's the time to come clean," Madeline said.

Ryker just looked at her. "If you're with the FBI, then contact my lawyer. Otherwise, fuck off."

Madeline stood, sniffing as she wiped at her nose. She was definitely on something.

"I'm going to give you time to think. I'll have Jerry—Special Agent Osborn take you back to your cell."

"Contact my lawyer," he said, as she left the room.

By the time Jerry returned, Ryker had had enough. The kid was so green he didn't even know how to secure a prisoner for transport back to his cell. Of course, Ryker had been playing the clueless card every time he interacted with the kid, so it wasn't entirely his fault. As soon as they'd reached his cell, Ryker took charge. Jerry was unconscious before he ever knew what hit him.

17

KAT

"Finally you decided to get out of the bed," Rip said. He was in the kitchen making a sandwich for lunch. Kat stuck up her middle finger. She'd only taken a small nap, not wallowed in self-pity all day. She needed a cup of coffee before trying to deal with him.

Kat had to get out of the house, run some errands, and get her life back on track. Mr. Sexy had been an awesome lay. She had no reason to regret what happened and it wasn't her fault that he thought she was a hooker. Kat could get over this and move on. Not that that meant she was going to check in on the dating site anytime soon. She really didn't want to hear how well Gandalf-22 made out with the real escort. He'd either want another date or turn her in for soliciting.

"I have to go out. I want to stop by the bistro. I lost one of my earrings last night and I want to see if anyone turned it in," Kat said. "But coffee first." Kat dropped in her favorite coffee pod and hit brew.

"Going back to the scene of the crime, I see," Rip joked.

"Ha ha, very funny. I have some other errands to run. I'm swinging by there just to check—I know it's unlikely, but I need to face the big bad world sometime," Kat said, turning away so her bright eyes wouldn't give her away. "And I wouldn't call the restaurant the scene of the crime, that would be the Greyson, thank you very much."

Kat was trying to laugh it off, but it would be a while before the thought of what happened didn't make her emotional.

Rip came up behind her, circling his big arms around her in a bear hug. "It was his loss. To think he could have gotten it for free."

"Jackass," Kat joked.

"Want me to come with?" Rip asked. "I can toss the sandwich and we could go out for food."

Kat had to do this herself. She couldn't lean on Rip the whole time. "Don't worry about it. I'm not hungry."

She needed to make sure she could get back out there in the real world and not freak out the minute someone spoke to her. Kat had to feel safe in her own skin. Taking Rip with her wouldn't prove that to herself. And she had to get up for work on Monday. Life had to go on. This was just a mini test before the workweek started.

"Do you need anything at the drugstore or the market?" Kat asked.

Rip shook his head. "Nothing, babe. I've got plans later so depending on how long you take I may not be here when you get back. Will you be okay?"

Kat turned in Rip's embrace, giving him a hug. "I'm good. I'll be fine. Don't worry about me. I'm gonna finish reading that murder mystery I've been meaning to read for like six weeks. So have fun and don't worry."

"As long as you're sure."

"I am."

18

JAYDA

Jayda's hair was still pink, but she could do nothing about it now. The temporary dye would eventually wash out. Until then, she was stuck. She took an Uber from the hotel to a coffee shop two blocks from the bistro. Jayda did a quick Internet search before leaving the hotel. Smith's body had been found, but was still unidentified. Apparently, the fire hadn't destroyed everything, which was par for the course for this cursed assignment.

Jayda donned a full-face balaclava before approaching the back door to the bistro. It was still early enough that only a handful of servers and staff were in the kitchen preparing for tonight's evening shift.

"No deliveries today," a man in a chef's coat said as she entered.

Jayda shot him with her silenced gun, dropping him where he stood.

Another kitchen worker was at the sink washing a pot. He cursed in Spanish just as Jayda dropped him. Three more died before she found the manager's office.

"Who the fuck are you?" he screamed as she rushed him.

Shoving the gun into his neck, she forced him to stay seated at his desk. "I want answers. If I like what I hear, then you'll live, otherwise you die."

"Okay, okay. Don't kill me. I don't want to die."

"Good. Now, first, you will text your workers and tell them to stay home tonight. Say the health inspector has shut the place down."

"I can't..." he tried to argue.

Jayda took the gun and shot him in the leg. He screamed. "I tell you what to do and you do it," Jayda said. "You don't, then people die."

"Holy fuck, okay, okay."

Jayda watched as the manager took out his phone. He selected several names for a group text.

> MANAGER: Don't come in—we've been shut down by the health inspectors. Let everyone know

Jayda took his phone and tossed it on the desk. Three or four pings for incoming texts sounded.

"Now, I want you to kill the video for today and Saturday night," Jayda said.

There was a pause. Jayda pressed her gun into the manager's leg. He cried out from the pain.

"Was my request not clear?" Jayda asked.

"I can't. I mean I can get rid of today's footage, but yesterday is already in the cloud."

"Bring up the app."

The manager pointed toward the computer. Jayda let him access the desktop. Clicking the keys, he logged in. Bringing up a surveillance app, he showed her the existing feed.

"I can kill it from here, just by turning it off," the manager said, selecting a menu and picking shutdown.

The system prompted to archive or delete the existing footage. The manager clicked delete.

"Okay, now go to the cloud storage," Jayda directed.

"I can't. I don't have the password."

"Call the person who has it and get it."

"The owner won't give it to me," the manager said.

"Roger," a female voice said from the dining room. "Are you back there?"

"It's the hostess. Let me tell her to go home."

Jayda rolled her eyes. This guy was an idiot. He couldn't delete the cloud footage. He was useless. Taking her gun, she shot him in the head. He slumped over in his chair. Jayda removed her balaclava and headed to the dining room. The same young blonde woman from last evening was headed toward the manager's office.

"What were you doing in the back?" she asked. "Hey, weren't you here last night?"

Jayda pulled out her gun. "That mistake will cost you."

"I don't know anything," she said.

"That is painfully obvious. Back to the podium. Perhaps I'll just leave you tied up." Jayda motioned the girl back with her gun.

With hands raised the hostess returned to the front. Jayda ordered her to get on her knees. Once down, Jayda shot the girl in the head, letting her body fall behind the podium.

Jayda returned to the manager's office. Searching the desk, she hoped to find a way to login to the remote cloud server. She'd noticed a Dropbox icon on the desktop, but clicking on it required a password be entered.

Dammit. Nothing was working out as expected. She reached for her phone. She'd get her tech guy to hack the account. Then she remembered she was already losing money on this gig, and the hacker wasn't cheap. She'd try finding the owner first. She took the manager's phone, unlocking it with his thumbprint. Scrolling through the contacts, she didn't see anyone's name that might be the owner of the restaurant. She should have asked for the owner's name before killing the manager. Giving up on that she tried Google. She searched: "Who owns Byron's Bistro in NYC?"

A noise from the front dining room startled Jayda. Was this another worker coming in after the texts were sent out to stay home? Fuck.

Jayda abandoned her search and returned to the door that led to the dining room.

"Hello," a young woman called out. "Hello? Is anyone here?"

19

KAT

After her coffee, Kat opted to avoid make up and just put on eyeliner and mascara. Her hair was pulled back into a ponytail. Physically, she looked normal, mentally she wasn't back to her pre-mistaken-for-an-escort self, but she didn't feel like a total failure as she made her way to the subway.

Kat's phone buzzed. It was a text from Rip.

RIP: Plans changed. I'll be back by seven. Want to catch a movie?
KAT: Not tonight
RIP: Pick up microwave popcorn, we'll binge watch something on Netflix
KAT: Okay

Kat couldn't just go back to bed. She needed to socialize, or work on Monday was going to suck more than usual.

The subway ride was quick, but stressful. The noise of the train and the half empty car felt claustrophobic, but she kept it together.

Kat had tried calling Byron's, but no one answered. She knew they opened in an hour, so there had to be someone onsite that could check their lost and found. Even if the location was closed, she needed the time away from the apartment.

The bistro was two blocks from the subway. As she neared, it looked empty, but she tried the door anyway. It opened.

Kat stepped inside. It was eerily quiet especially compared to last evening when the place was packed. There was a stale smell to the air that Kat hadn't noticed before. Maybe the cleaners hadn't finished yet or maybe once the kitchen started cooking the smells would cover any lingering odor.

"Hello," Kat called out. "Hello? Is anyone here?"

Most of the lights were still off, but Kat knew someone had to be in the restaurant or why else would the door be open. If it hadn't been bright outside this would've been creepy as fuck. Not that the place looked like an abandoned asylum or anything. It was a posh New York City bistro.

Kat stepped up to the hostess podium. She tried calling out one more time, but there was still no answer. She heard a noise from the back. Was that a door closing? Maybe someone was there.

"Hello," Kat said, stepping around the podium to head towards the noise.

In the split second that it took her to register the dead body of the hostess laying at her feet, she thought, *maybe this is a stupid plan and I should come back when they are open.* Once her brain connected the dead body with her creepy as fuck situation, she screamed.

That was when she heard the gunshot and, as if it were a movie, she swore she felt a puff of wind just before something slammed into the wood of the podium beside her. In silent panic, she realized that the gunshot she'd heard, and the puff of air she'd felt, and the thunk as something hit the wooden podium beside her, could only mean one thing. Someone had aimed a bullet at her—and missed.

Move move move. She screamed at herself to react. It seemed to take forever for her body to obey the command. Another shot was fired as Kat turned to run. A searing hot pain kissed the skin of her arm, just before the glass front door shattered. Reaching around she grabbed her arm, feeling the sticky sensation of fresh blood. Instinctively, she realized she'd been shot. What the fuck was happening?

Out on the sidewalk, a woman walking with her friend screamed as the door shattered. "Call 911!"

Kat ducked behind the podium trying to avoid any other bullets. She heard at least one other shot, but wasn't sure where it hit.

The woman from outside yelled, "The cops are on their way."

Kat's heart was beating a mile a minute. She was paralyzed with fear but her mind was sharp as a tack at the same time. It was like this was all happening to someone else and she was watching it from a safe place, only she wasn't safe—she was being shot at by someone inside Byron's who had already killed at least one person. Kat didn't want to think about the fact that a restaurant this busy would've had a full kitchen staff here by now, with at least one manager, and probably a few of the wait staff to get the dining room ready.

Was everyone dead—except her?

Kat pulled out her phone, muted it, and texted Rip.

KAT: At Byron's Bistro, shots fired, still pinned
RIP: WTF, are you serious?
KAT: YES
RIP: I'm near. Calling cops. Stay down. Fuck
RIP: I'm coming and I love you
RIP: Don't die...why aren't you answering?
KAT: I'm here, hurry

In the distance Kat heard sirens blaring. Thank God they were getting closer. She heard more noise from the back. A couple of doors slamming and foot falls running away, then nothing. She didn't move. She'd stay exactly where she was until the police arrived.

Kat checked her arm. It was just a small graze. There was blood, and it hurt like hell but she'd make it. At least she was no longer worrying about Mr. Sexy. Of course, she wasn't sure a traumatic event was really the way to forget about him either, but maybe that was her thing now. One crazy insane experience after another.

At least she wasn't dead.

20

JAYDA

"Fuck, fuck, fuck," Jayda said under her breath as she hurried down the alley away from the bistro.

Could this job go any more wrong? At least she'd taken care of today's footage, but last night's video surveillance was still in the fucking cloud.

She could have waited to kill the manager. With more pressure he would have at least attempted to contact the owner, but then the hostess had arrived and his time was up. Now the police would have a reason to care about this restaurant. Fuck, and that little bitch that came in at the end. She fucked things up. Jayda had planned to start a fire in the kitchen, but she'd heard a passerby shouting she had called the police. Jayda couldn't risk them catching her.

Exiting the alley on the other side of the restaurant, Jayda shoved her balaclava into her messenger bag. The police would eventually find the footage, but there had been another redhead there that night—same dress and hairstyle. Her double might be mistaken as the one that walked out with Smith. At this point it likely didn't matter. Jayda would kill Greyson tomorrow, then take out Ana when she met to pick up her cash payment. She wondered if Fedor, Ana's bodyguard, would be a problem, but she'd cross that bridge later.

Sirens sounded in the distance. Jayda slowed her walk. She couldn't risk looking suspicious so near the crime scene. Removing her outer jacket, she turned it inside out and tied it around her waist. It was reversible. One side matte black, the other side a vibrant red. The red side was out now, giving her a completely different look than the girl that had entered the restaurant half an hour ago.

Jayda circled back around the block. People had started gathering outside the bistro. Jayda slid on her sunglasses, hiding in plain site within the crowd of onlookers.

A cop car was already on site. Two cops entered the building, guns at the ready. Jayda could hear other sirens approaching. The bistro was about to get very busy.

Within seconds another cop car screeched to a halt. Two more officers were on the scene. One of the first cops returned from the restaurant, with the young woman Jayda had shot at in tow. She was the reason Jayda's perfectly good arson had turned into an instantly recognizable massacre. A fire might have tagged this as an accident and delayed discovery of the real cause of death. Now it would be a full-blown homicide investigation.

Jayda studied the girl. She looked shaken, but otherwise unharmed. Damn, none of Jayda's shots had hit anything important.

Animatedly the girl waved her hand at the restaurant then at her sleeve, which was covered in blood. Her hair, pulled back in a ponytail, swished back and forth, the red gleaming brightly in the sun.

"Red hair," Jayda muttered. She hadn't noticed that before.

Jayda focused on the woman's face. Was this the girl from last night? Had she come back to ask about the date that never happened? That would be weird, but then why else was she here? If it was her.

Jayda took in the girl's appearance. She was the right height. With a blue dress and her hair twisted in a chignon, she could easily be the woman from last night.

Jayda moved around to position herself closer to the girl as she talked to the cops.

The police officer was speaking. "You stopped by to see if they found your earring?"

"Yes. I tried to call, but no one answered. I had errands to run, so I just decided to stop by. The hostess was dead."

"Yes, ma'am," the officer said.

"Kat, my name is Kat," the woman said, her voice still shaky.

"Okay, Kat. We're going to get the paramedics to look you over. Then we have a few more questions."

"Okay."

The woman, Kat, was led to the side as two more police officers arrived. An older cop stumbled out the door of the bistro, puking on the sidewalk. One of the arriving officers started placing barricades to keep the pedestrians from getting too close. The sirens of the first ambulance to arrive blared as it pulled to a stop. Most of the crowd had their phones up. A man to Jayda's right was live streaming on social media. News crews were starting to gather. It was turning into a circus.

Jayda scanned the crowd. Could she make her way to Kat, pretend to be a paramedic, and finish her off? No, too risky. Too many witnesses and no time to get the necessary disguise. As Jayda prepared to leave, she noticed a tall man with sunglasses staring at her from the crowd on the other side. And damnit all to hell, she recognized him. It was West, the real West, not the man child she'd killed last night or the agent that met with Greyson today.

What was he doing here?

"Kat, Kat," a sexy young guy yelled, trying to get past the cops.

"Who are you?" the officer asked.

"Rip Taylor. That's my roommate," he said, pointing at Kat.

Jayda took out her phone and snapped pics of Kat and her roommate. She could get one of her hacker friends to find them on social media. Jayda glanced back toward West, but he was gone.

Turning on her heel, she left the scene.

She'd drop by Greyson's office tomorrow and kill him, then she'd need to disappear, quickly, until this all blew over.

BISHOP

Bishop was back at his hotel. He opened the message app on his phone to text Madeline.

BISHOP: Greyson meeting uneventful. Have second meeting scheduled tomorrow at 10 AM. We need to talk

Greyson had spent most of the brunch focused on idle chitchat, no business. Bishop kept his answers simple, realizing quickly that this was a get to know the prospective client session and very little business would be discussed. In one way, it took the pressure off the meeting, but also left the door open to not being asked for a follow up sit down. Greyson must have been convinced by Bishop's impersonation, because he eagerly invited Bishop to meet the following day at his office to discuss what CGH could do for Volkov.

Bishop hadn't been able to get the news about Sarah Daniels out of his mind. Drake had asked Bishop to look into it, but it hadn't been a federal case. He'd never told Drake, but Bishop had asked one of his buddies on the force to review the details. No mention of unidentified fingerprints had been discussed. Of course, they probably weren't the only set in Bacon's car, which meant statistically they were irrelevant. But for them to match Ryker made no logical sense. It put all kinds of thoughts in Bishop's head about Sarah's death. Had it been accidental? Bishop couldn't think about this now. He put it on the back burner until he had a chance to ask Madeline what she found out in the interrogation.

Bishop checked his phone. He was surprised Madeline hadn't texted back. Then he noticed there were a few texts on the group chat with Jerry and Madeline, and a single text from Jerry. Bishop clicked over to read the group chat first.

> JERRY: Should I investigate Edward Watson Esquire? Ryker's lawyer?
> MADELINE: I told you not to listen to the recording. Leave it alone. I'm handling it
> JERRY: Sorry…I thought you'd want me to transcribe it
> MADELINE: No, move Ryker back to his holding cell

Bishop checked the time and noticed the texts were from a couple of hours ago, while he was still in the meeting with Greyson. Bishop clicked over to Jerry's message.

> JERRY: I'll meet you in interrogation room B, but you better have your story straight or I'm going to Reece

What the fuck was Jerry talking about? Was this another text for Madeline? No, this one was on their private chat. What the fuck ever. The kid could take anything he wanted to Reece. Jerry had to be talking about the email he'd told him to forward. Madeline hadn't told Bishop to ask for it, but there wasn't anything private about it. It was relevant to the case that they were all working. He wouldn't even dignify Jerry's text with a response.

Bishop considered calling Madeline, but opted to check his

email, social media, and news sites first. He'd been playing Ryker West all afternoon and he needed to touch base with his real self and see what was going on in the world. Madeline could call him if she wanted an update.

He scanned through his FBI email first. He had an interesting response from Reece, the NYC ADIC, about the email he'd sent explaining his suspicion that a concierge at the Red Martini might be dealing drugs on the side. Reece wanted to know what Bishop was doing at the Red Martini. Reece questioned if Greyson was at the bar, or was it another person of interest Bishop was surveilling?

Bishop wasn't sure what to make of Reece's questions. He'd given Reece a heads up that a concierge might be running drugs, but he hadn't tied it to Greyson or anything to do with the case. Was Reece not aware he was undercover as Ryker West and as part of that cover he'd had to take out the escort? Madeline had secured the money to tip the call girl, and Reece would have had to sign the requisition form. Reece had to know about the escort.

Bishop brought up the original email to determine if he'd misstated the situation at the bar. The email looked fine. He noticed he hadn't copied his own boss or Madeline, but for something like this it wasn't necessary. Bishop flagged the email to discuss with Madeline before he replied to Reece. It wasn't anything urgent so he didn't feel the need to call today. It could wait until Monday.

Bishop noticed an email from Alex on his personal account.

TO: Scott Bishop
FROM: Alex Wren
SUBJECT: Blast from the past
Bro,
When did you sport a beard?
https://www.laverdad.es/.../201412/29/masacre-en-boda-
   20141229235956-v.html

Alex

Bishop pasted the link into a private browser window. An article displayed showing a chaotic scene from the Wedding Party Massacre. A daughter of Jose Ortega had almost been killed and two groomsmen were killed, when her wedding was crashed by a rival cartel. The Ortegas took swift revenge, killing many from other cartels who had attended the wedding as supposed allies. Anyone they suspected of being involved was eliminated. Drake's girl, Haden, had been at the wedding, but this was a scene of the aftermath. Bishop studied the picture more closely. What had Alex expected him to see?

Holy shit—it was the real Ryker West. How the hell did Alex find this picture? And what was West, in standard Army Ranger black ops body gear, doing at the Wedding Party Massacre? Was this guy connected to General Davis?

Bishop retrieved his secure FBI phone from his overnight bag and brought up General Davis's contact information, then texted two words.

BISHOP: Ryker West

Bishop waited for a minute, then texted.

BISHOP: The Wedding Party Massacre

Bishop saw the typing bubbles form near Davis's name. A few seconds later, a single word appeared.

DAVIS: FUBAR

Bishop's phone rang. It was a secure line with a blocked number. He answered the call.

"Yes, sir," Bishop answered, assuming it was Davis.

"You don't make it easy, do you, son," General John Davis said. "I thought after that cluster you and the boys just got into, you'd have enough sense to stay out of old military ops. Now you're asking me about a dead man."

"Ryker West isn't dead, but for the moment I'll assume you already know that. Why would he be working for Vasili Volkov?"

General Davis's rough laugh sounded like ground stones. "I'm not at liberty to discuss certain particulars, but you should back off and leave it be. I tell you that as a friend, not as your former commander."

Bishop wasn't sure what Davis meant by that. Did he actually know what Ryker was doing and couldn't say, or was Ryker a deserter? Had Ryker switched sides to work for Volkov? No, Davis wouldn't be so coy if a man he'd trusted had defected.

"How does a dead man still have an active warrant in Texas?" Bishop asked. "Or have his partial prints found connected to a drunk driving case in Chicago?"

"Above my pay grade."

Fuck, what was above General Davis's pay grade? Another black ops mission? Another agency?

"I may be in too far on this one to walk away," Bishop said.

The real Ryker West was in FBI custody waiting for transport to Texas for an old warrant and Bishop was pretending to be West —so yeah, he was too far into this to leave it be. Even if Greyson offered some sort of illegal deal, what did the FBI have? If Ryker was undercover with—who? The CIA, NSA, some other shady government organization?—what did that mean? How did Vasili Volkov fit into this? How did Greyson fit into this? How did Sarah Daniels fit into this?

Did Madeline know?

"Like I said, son. Don't get in his way. He's not the man you think he is," Davis said, then disconnected the call.

"Not the man I think he is," Bishop said to himself. "Fucking hell."

It had to be the CIA. NSA wouldn't need a field agent with Ryker West's credentials, but the CIA could place a double agent in with the bad guys. Something to do with the State Department? Maybe they wanted the right bad guy in charge of a small country or province. So why was Ryker here to launder money through Greyson? The FBI wanted Greyson out of the money laundering business, but it had no plans to prosecute Volkov. What else could be happening, if it wasn't Volkov? Was Ryker here for something else?

Ana Ivanov.

The FBI hadn't known anything about her involvement with Greyson, but that didn't mean the CIA hadn't known. Bishop had to talk with Madeline. He had to find out what she knew. This assignment was originally surveillance only. Who had actually signed off on changing it to an undercover sting? Did Reece know what Madeline was doing?

Bishop dialed Madeline's number. It went straight to voicemail. He disconnected the call. A text came in from Madeline.

MADELINE: No time to talk
BISHOP: We need to talk. Ryker may not be what he seems
MADELINE: It's handled. Stay in character. Record the meet with Greyson. We'll talk after
BISHOP: What's been handled? Is he CIA? Is this a dual agency op?

A few seconds passed with no response.

BISHOP: Madeline, what the fuck is going on?

The typing bubbles finally appeared.

MADELINE: Stay in character. I'll debrief you tomorrow after your meeting with Greyson

MADELINE: Don't fuck this up, Scott

Bishop shook his head. What the fuck did she think he'd fuck up? Bishop didn't like where this was going, but he wouldn't break cover because Madeline was being Madeline. She'd gotten her tough as nails reputation for a reason. He switched topics.

BISHOP: Did you see Reece's email?
MADELINE: Everything is under control. Focus on your part, Scott. Close the deal with Greyson. Let me worry about Reece and Ryker

Bishop wanted to ask about Sarah Daniels, but if Ryker was CIA the odds were good that Sarah Daniels was another case and wouldn't be connected to Greyson. He'd wait and see where this was going before he tried to bring Sarah into the conversation. He also thought about asking Madeline to rein in Jerry, but that fight wasn't worth it. He'd let it go until after the Greyson meeting tomorrow. If she continued to lock him out, then he'd go to Reece. Bishop replied to Madeline.

BISHOP: Roger that

Bishop left his phone on the dresser and picked up the room service menu. He wanted to order a beer but didn't want the hassle of having to justify it on his expense report. Bishop flipped on the TV and considered taking a nap while he waited for his food.

Bishop's phone chirped with an incoming text. Getting up, he grabbed his phone. It was from Alex.

ALEX: Yo, delete that email
BISHOP: It's nothing. Don't worry about it

ALEX: Meghan ran it up the flagpole and almost got fired. You never saw it
BISHOP: Fired? WTF
ALEX: And I almost got reassigned. Just delete the email… because there are some scary dudes that don't want that picture circulated
ALEX: Who the fuck is Ryker West?

Bishop considered not answering Alex, but it wasn't fair to keep it a secret. He could just as easily have called General Davis and gotten the same information Bishop had.

BISHOP: CIA I think…Davis wouldn't tell me, said it was above his pay grade
ALEX: Fucking hell…just delete the email, okay
BISHOP: 10-4

If Bishop hadn't been sure before, he was now. "Scary dudes" and Meghan almost getting fired had CIA stamped all over it. Bishop opened his laptop. The tab with the article was still up. He right-clicked to save the image, but he got an image not found error. He moved the error dialog box out of the way and snapped a screenshot of his browser window. Clicking over to his email, he deleted Alex's message.

Bishop ran his hand through his hair. There was no way Madeline had looped in the CIA, or she would have never been allowed to pick up Ryker. Now he was pretending to be Ryker and he had no fucking clue what their mission was—assuming it was a CIA mission and not some generic cover work Ryker was doing to set up a new money launderer for Volkov.

Bishop had to text Madeline. She had to handle this tonight.

BISHOP: Ryker is CIA. Contact his handler and explain what we are doing

MADELINE: They are onboard. Stay in character. We'll talk tomorrow after the op
BISHOP: As always your communication with the team is stellar

What a bitch. Bishop tossed his phone on the dresser. He was done for the night. A knock at the door sounded. Good, his food was here.

22

KAT

"Now, Ms. Fox, why would you be lying about this?" the detective asked.

Lying about what? Kat thought. She explained like twenty times already that she'd stopped by the restaurant to see if they'd found her earring. Yes, she tried to call first. No, no one had answered. At this point it was just getting ridiculous. Kat tried to remember what the detective's name was. He was a tall, lanky guy with black hair, balding and middle-aged. It was something with an M—Montgomery.

"Mr. Montgomery, I'm sorry, Detective Montgomery, I'm not lying. I went to the restaurant to see if anyone had turned in a small diamond stud earring. That's it. I have absolutely no clue who would have wanted to come in and shoot up the place."

"Ms. Fox, why exactly were you at Byron's Bistro last evening?"

Kat had to stop herself from rolling her eyes. "I was there to have dinner with a friend."

"You see, that's where there's a bit of a problem in your story. You've yet to tell me who this friend is. And quite frankly it's becoming more and more obvious that you don't want to tell me who they are."

Kat didn't want to tell this guy about West. She wanted to forget it ever fucking happened. She also didn't want to get into the whole blind date fiasco. Especially if that guy wound up with the actual escort. She still hadn't checked in on her account to see if he left a comment. This was getting ridiculous but Kat didn't want to make up a name. She would stick to the bare minimum facts about the situation. The detective didn't have to know that West thought she was a hooker. He didn't have to know that she was there to meet someone else, or that she'd actually signed up for a dating service and not done the whole swipe right thing like everyone else. It was just a new acquaintance. A random blind date.

"I didn't realize my social life was going to be put on display. It was a blind date. His name was West. We went out dancing after," Kat said, shrugging her shoulder like it had been no big deal.

Detective Montgomery tilted his head as if studying Kat to determine if she was being truthful. It was a little bit creepy. But she couldn't exactly go off the rails and start screaming. She didn't want them to think that she had something to do with the shooting. She just wanted to go home and be done with this whole day. The detective opened his mouth to say something, but was interrupted when another detective stuck her head in the door.

"Jimmy, we've got an ID on the victim from the warehouse. Jersey pulled fingerprints off the mint wrapper found in the victim's pocket. Also, the techs have confirmed that today's video at the bistro was wiped. We have a call in for the owner to hand over the code for their video backups," the female detective said. "I'll let you know when we have it."

Detective Jimmy Montgomery nodded. "What's the name of our victim?"

"Last name Smith, lives in East Village."

The female detective passed Montgomery a picture of a bearded guy. It looked like a social media profile pic and kind of reminded Kat of a bearded Mr. Sexy. She really needed to stop thinking about him.

"Has Detective Flores contacted next of kin yet?" Montgomery asked.

"Flores is asking for an assist," the detective said. "He agrees with you. He thinks the two cases are related."

"Yeah, Jen, tell Flores I'm in. I'm almost done here. I'll be out in a minute," Montgomery said.

The second detective left the room, closing the door behind her. Detective Montgomery turned back to Kat.

"Don't leave town, Ms. Fox. I might have more questions for you later."

Kat couldn't get out of there fast enough. She found Rip waiting for her at the front of the station. She shook her head so he wouldn't say anything until after they left the building. Pulling up her ride share app, she summoned an Uber to take her back to her apartment. She just didn't want to deal with the subway.

"What the fuck happened? Did they interrogate you?" Rip asked. "Why the hell were you in there so long talking to them? Was it about the dead body they found in New Jersey?"

"Stop, stop," Kat said. "I have no clue why he kept me so long. I think they got suspicious because I wasn't coming clean with the whole blind date clusterfuck. It's not like I was going to tell them the guy I had dinner with thought I was a hooker."

"True."

"But why would *you* think I had anything to do with a dead body found in New Jersey?"

Rip chuckled. "I was just fucking with you. I heard two cops saying the evidence with the fingerprint had Byron's Bistro logo on it. I guess this guy was last seen at the bistro on Saturday night, and they're all in a tizzy now thinking the murders today are related to him."

"The dead guy was at the bistro Saturday night?"

"Yeah, but it hasn't made the news yet," Rip said.

"That's what they meant," Kat said, remembering what the second detective said. She thought back to their conversation. At the time Kat hadn't realized they meant the murders at the bistro were connected to the dead guy from the warehouse.

"What are you talking about?" Rip asked.

"Another detective came into the interrogation room and updated Montgomery about a body found in a warehouse in New Jersey, some guy named Smith who lives in East Village. Anyway, they also said the video footage from the bistro for today was wiped and they were planning to get the archived footage…" Fuck, they were looking for last night's footage, when Kat was there eating dinner with West. Smith looked like a bearded West. Did Smith still have the beard? If not, were they going to think she was with Smith? Let's hope she didn't need an alibi, because she had no desire to track down West.

"What's wrong?" Rip asked.

Kat exhaled a long breath. "Nothing. I just want to get home and put this day behind me." Kat's phone buzzed. The Uber was almost there.

"How's your arm? The paramedics said it wasn't bad," Rip said.

Kat looked down at the wrapping. It was going to be a little sore for a few days while it healed, but she just had to keep it clean and bandaged so no big deal.

"It's fine. The Tylenol is working," Kat said. Spotting the silver sedan listed on her ride share app, she said, "Oh, good, there's the Uber."

Rip was quiet on the way to the apartment. Kat leaned her head back on the seat. She just wanted to take a nap but she wasn't going to do that in the backseat of a random Uber. Not even with Rip there to protect her.

"Thanks for being there today," Kat said. "I can't even imagine having to go home to an empty apartment."

Rip put his arms around Kat.

"Come here, Kit Kat, snuggle with me."

Kat let Rip hold her in his arms. She felt safe with him.

Rip helped Kat up the stairs and into bed. Then lay beside her until she fell asleep.

23

KAT

Monday started way too early for Kat's liking. She walked into her office building more or less ready for the day to be over. A balloon delivery person with pink hair was arguing with front desk security.

Shoving her balloons in his face, she said, "Look, dude, I've got a schedule to keep. Just look up the name."

Kat ignored the situation and headed for the elevator bank. Considering everyone in this building was a stuffed shirt, she was sure the delivery was meant for a different building. Gold and pink balloons with a fluffy pink bear just didn't fit. Of course, it could be for one of the admins, but who would want that hideous thing on their desk?

Kat pressed the call button and waited. A few more people gathered behind her. She pressed the call button again but knew it wouldn't speed the elevator.

"Oh, great," a man behind her said. "Elevator maintenance again today?"

"I hope not," a woman said. "Friday sucked."

Kat had heard about the elevator issues Friday but building maintenance had sent out an update indicating everything was back to normal. Two dings sounded and two doors opened at the same time. Kat entered the nearest car. The walls were covered with thick blankets.

"Who's moving in?" a woman asked.

"Investment banker on eight," another woman said.

"The service elevator must be down again," someone grumbled.

Kat tuned out the complaints about the elevator, which had been slower than normal for about a week. She tapped her badge on the elevator panel and pressed the seven button.

It would be another half hour before Mr. Greyson would be in the office. She considered asking Mr. Greyson if she could leave early today. Rip had stuffed the cash she'd gotten from West into an envelope to be dropped off at the no-kill shelter a few blocks from her office. She'd planned to go by there this morning but was running late. Maybe she'd go at lunch. The sooner she got rid of the money the better she'd feel. Until then, she'd have to keep her purse close. Rip said he'd come by for lunch if she wanted him to, which meant they could go together. Kat would check her calendar, then text Rip. Her grand idea to not bring her lunch today hadn't factored in her boss's calendar, but she'd cheated death yesterday so come hell or high water she was going out for lunch.

Kat sat down at her desk and logged in. She checked her emails. There was one from Mr. Greyson about a new meeting that he wanted added to his calendar this morning at 10 AM. She was to block an hour of his time and cancel anything else that he might have booked. This was not an unusual request after a weekend of social engagements. She rarely scheduled anything before lunch on a Monday for this very reason. Today there was nothing to move, although he did have lunch plans with Ms. Ivanov. Kat added Mr. Greyson's appointment from 10 AM to 11 AM. She notified the front desk and Ericka in reception to expect a visitor. No attendance list was provided, so Kat assumed it was a private meeting. She placed an order for pastries, to be delivered from the corner deli at 9:50.

Kat took out her phone to text Rip.

KAT: Lunch is a go, be here at noon
RIP: OK...is all good?
KAT: So far

Kat wasn't sure all would ever be good again, but it was Monday. Maybe by Friday she'd feel differently.

Mr. Greyson arrived at his normal time. Kat prepared his coffee and delivered his morning paper.

"Is everything set for ten?" Mr. Greyson asked.

"Yes, sir," Kat answered. "What name should I give to reception?"

"Mr. West."

Kat momentarily lost her train of thought.

"Are you alright, Miss Fox?"

"Yes. Sorry. I knew a guy named West—never mind. Will there be anything else, sir?" Kat asked, silently admonishing herself for losing it over a guy with the same name as Mr. Sexy.

"Call and get me a reservation at Tony's for lunch."

"Yes, sir."

Kat left Mr. Greyson's office before she said something else stupid. Her boss didn't care about his employee's social life, and there was no way in hell she was going to mention her one-night stand with the guy that thought she was a hooker.

After making the reservation, she updated the ten o'clock meeting with Mr. West's name.

Kat's phone buzzed with a text from Rip.

RIP: Need to cancel. See you at home later
KAT: OK...no worries. See you tonight

Kat was bummed that Rip had cancelled, but she remembered him mentioning a job interview, so maybe he'd gotten a call back. Kat checked the time. It was almost ten. She needed to hit the restroom before the meeting started. She dialed Ericka, the seventh-floor receptionist.

"Seventh floor," Ericka answered.

"Hey, it's Kat. Can you bring the pastries to the conference room when they get here? I need to make a quick pit stop before Mr. Greyson's 10 AM arrives."

"Sure, no problem. Hey, who sent the balloons?"

Kat assumed Ericka was talking about the delivery she'd seen at the front desk this morning. "No clue. Now I have to go—literally."

Kat ended the call, grabbed her purse, which still held the money she planned to donate to the shelter, and headed to the ladies room. As she turned the corner, a woman dressed in a black business suit ran into Kat.

"Watch it," the woman said, pushing her way past.

Startled, Kat stepped aside. The rude woman with a chignon of pink hair disappeared around the corner.

Pink hair. What a weird trend, Kat thought as she beelined to the restroom.

After taking care of business, she stood at the sink washing her hands. Kat jumped when one of the toilets auto flushed. She'd been sure she was alone in the washroom. Kat looked under the stalls. No one was there. Then the toilet auto flushed again.

"Is someone here?" Kat asked the empty room.

To free her hands, Kat slung her crossbody bag over her head. Steeling her nerves, she pushed open each stall door one at a time.

"Hello?" she said, giving her would-be lurker one more chance to speak up.

Reaching her hand toward the last stall door, she gave it a quick shove.

Pop. Bang. Flush.

"What the fuck!" Kat freaked, flashing back to her ordeal yesterday at the restaurant as the door bounced back toward her.

The squeak of multiple objects rustling together behind the stall door pulled Kat back from her fear. Above the stall, a pink balloon bobbed into view. "Ohmygod," Kat said, laughing as she clutched her chest.

She pushed the stall door open, slowly this time. The balloons Kat had seen this morning were tied to the back of the toilet. The ribbon was tripping the auto flush sensor, and someone had stuffed the plush bear into the bowl. Kat pulled out the bear and untied the ribbon. She'd need to call building maintenance when she got back to her desk.

Kat tossed the soaked bear into the trash, which was when she noticed it was full of clothes.

"What a mess," she muttered, then remembered the delivery woman from this morning. "Pink hair isn't a trend."

With the balloons trailing behind her, Kat hurried back to her desk. She dialed security.

"Security," a gruff male voice answered.

"Hi, this is Kaitlyn Fox on seven. I believe a delivery person the front desk let up is roaming around the building unescorted. She's now in business attire. Her delivery outfit is in the trash in the ladies restroom."

"When did you see her last?"

"About five minutes ago."

"Okay. We'll send someone up to investigate. Call back if you see her again."

"Thank you," Kat said, then hung up.

"Nice balloons," a charmingly half British-half American voice said.

Kat's heart skipped a beat. How the hell was Greyson's 10 AM her Mr. Sexy? Looking up, she met the man's cool blue eyes. Blue, not gray—not her Mr. Sexy's eyes. She took a deep breath to calm down. At least the world hadn't gone completely crazy.

Kat took in the new Mr. West. He was broad shouldered, tall, and very handsome. He had dark blond hair and a close-cut beard. If not for the beard she thought he might be a dead ringer for her—no, not hers—for West.

"Twice in two days," she muttered.

Was she going to start seeing Mr. Sexy in every guy with blond hair that she met? She shook it off—the Smith guy from the police station photo had nothing to do with either West. Mr. Ten-O'clock was very attractive, but she had to pull it together and do her job. She clipped a magnetic document holder to the balloon ribbons, attaching them to her filing cabinet. She'd deal with them later.

"Can I help you?" she asked.

"Certainly, love. My name is Mr. West. I'm here to see Mr. Greyson."

"Yes, his ten o'clock," Kat said.

"Actually, I was supposed to meet with him yesterday for brunch. I was delayed, then lost my mobile. I'm hoping he can see me now."

"Oh," Kat said, a bit flustered.

"Do I know you?" he asked. "Have we met?"

"No. I'd remember you," Kat said, then winced. "Sorry, it's been a crazy week."

"It's only Monday, love."

Kat ignored his possible flirting and said, "So you're not the Mr. West he's meeting with today at ten?"

Kat checked the time. It was 9:59 AM. And now there was going to be a second Mr. West here any minute. Kat was starting to think she should have called in sick—she had been shot yesterday—okay, grazed—but it was a good excuse.

"No," the first Mr. West said.

"I'm sorry but Mr. Greyson has…" Kat stammered as the door to the office suite opened again. "What the fuck," she muttered, as

Mr. Sexy-Who-Thought-She-Was-A-Hooker-West strolled in. Seriously, how was this shit happening to her.

Mr. Sexy froze when their eyes met. She did a double take between the two Mr. Wests. They both had sandy blond hair, although on closer inspection new Mr. West's hair had a few more lighter streaks mixed in, and of course her Mr. Sexy didn't have a beard.

Bearded-West turned around to face Mr. Sexy.

Before Kat could compose herself and figure out what was going on, absolutely everything went to hell.

24

BISHOP

Bishop arrived with no time to spare for his 10 AM meeting with Greyson. After catching the tail end of a news report of the massacre at Byron's Bistro yesterday, he'd tried to contact Madeline before he left the hotel, but she wasn't answering her phone. He'd see her after the Greyson meeting. For now he had to stay in character and get the job done.

As he opened the door to the building, a frantic voice called out behind him.

"Hold the door, please."

Bishop held the door as a frazzled young woman carrying a box of pastries hurried toward him.

"Thanks!" she said, "The deli was supposed to deliver these, but they forgot and Greyson's meeting starts right now."

"Well, then, it's a good thing I'm late, love," he said with a smile.

"Oh, are you his ten o'clock?" she asked.

Bishop nodded.

The woman pointed toward the main reception desk, then halted. The desk was crawling with security. A tall man, slim build with black hair, in his mid-forties and balding, was at the desk.

Bishop watched as the man pulled out his identification, showing the security guards behind the desk a badge. He was a cop.

"That's weird," she said. "You can just follow me up. If I leave you down here you may never make it. The elevators have been slow as molasses all day."

"Thank you, Miss—?" Bishop asked.

"Ericka. Everyone just calls me Ericka," she said.

Bishop should check in at the front, but he didn't want scrutiny from local cops. Ryker West, entitled European moneyman to a wealthy underworld oligarch, wouldn't care about breaking the rules for building security, so Bishop let Ericka lead him toward the bank of elevators. Keeping an ear to the action at the front desk, Bishop listened as they waited for the lift.

"I'm here to see Ms. Fox," the cop said.

Bishop immediately thought of Kat, wishing he was here to see his Ms. Fox.

The cop continued. "She's wanted for some follow-up questioning."

"What kind of questioning?" the security guy asked.

"A man named Smith was murdered. She was at his last known location."

"So you're not the cops here to help with the intruder?" a different security guy asked.

"No, Bob," the first security guy said. "We just got the call five minutes ago."

The cop spoke up. "We're not here for that, but we're happy to assist."

The elevator came before Bishop had a chance to hear more. It would have been good to know where the intruder was last seen, but this wasn't his rodeo.

Ericka pressed the seven, but the elevator stopped on two. A young man entered the car.

In a stage whisper, he leaned in to speak with Ericka.

"Did you hear? Intruder on seven," the guy said.

"What? When did you hear that?" Ericka asked.

"Romeo, my boy toy in security just texted. Oh, and apparently some cops are here to talk to Foxy about a murder. They probably think she did it."

"What-the-fuck-ever," Ericka said, then blushed as she glanced back at Bishop. "You're making this shit up."

The elevator stopped on five. The young guy got off.

"No, I'm not," he said, just as the elevator doors closed.

"Sorry about that," Ericka said as she slapped the elevator button for seven again, as if that would speed things up.

"Who's Foxy?" Bishop asked.

"Ignore him. There is no way Greyson's administrative assistant is being questioned for murder. She's as boring as they come."

Bishop had heard the detective. It sounded like Ms. Fox was witness to a murder, not suspected of it. Then it registered what else Ericka had said. "I thought you were Mr. Greyson's assistant."

The elevator dinged and the doors opened up on the seventh floor.

"No, I'm just the seventh-floor receptionist." Pointing ahead, Ericka said, "See those doors? Just go straight through there. I'm going to drop these Danishes in the conference room."

"Thanks," Bishop said.

Fox, Bishop thought. Greyson has an assistant named Fox—and the escort he hired was also named Fox—weird.

Approaching the door, Bishop heard voices on the other side.

"I'm sorry but Mr. Greyson has…" Kat stammered to a halt as Bishop entered the room.

What the hell. Kat—Kat Fox. Ms. Fox was Greyson's assistant. The man Kat was speaking with turned to face Bishop.

Ryker West. CIA undercover, ex-black-ops Army Ranger, Ryker Fucking West.

Bishop saw the recognition in Ryker's eyes. Did he know Bishop was there pretending to be him? Bishop caught movement as Ryker drew his weapon. Kat screamed. Bishop raised his gun a half second later. What was going on? Why was West here?

A loud thump sounded from behind Greyson's door.

Before either man could do anything, Greyson's office door flew open. A woman darted out, silenced gun firing. Ryker dove for cover. A bullet ricocheted off the lamp on Kat's desk. She screamed again.

Bishop tackled Kat, blocking her body with his and taking cover behind her desk.

Ryker aimed and fired at the pink-haired woman but missed as she crashed through the suite doors. Bishop also raised his gun to return fire, but the attacker was already out of sight. There was no safe shot.

"What the fuck is going on," Kat screamed.

Pushing to his feet, Bishop told Kat, "Stay down." Leveling his gun on Ryker, he said, "Hands up."

"You don't sound like you," Kat said. "He sounds like you."

Fuck, he'd let his fake accent slip. Bishop stayed focused on Ryker. Kat's concerns would have to wait.

Ryker looked unimpressed. He didn't lower his weapon or raise his hands but he also didn't point his gun at Bishop.

Bishop's instincts were telling him to pursue the shooter, but he couldn't leave Kat here alone with Ryker. The guy had pulled a gun on an FBI agent. CIA or not, Bishop didn't have a reason to trust him.

Bishop took the phone from her desk and handed it to Kat. "I'm FBI Special Agent Scott Bishop," he said in his normal American accent. "Call the front desk. Tell them the intruder fired shots and is headed their way." He had no clue if the intruder had taken the elevator or the stairs, but for now that was the best he could do. Bishop returned his attention to Ryker. "How did you get out of FBI custody?"

Ryker laughed. In the rough British accent Bishop had tried to emulate, he said, "Was I ever in FBI custody? Seemed like a rogue agent and her lackey to me."

"Cut the act. Your CIA handlers are in communication with Madeline."

Ryker's left eyebrow raised. His accent, which had been significantly more British, sounded a bit more American now. "Madeline needs a stint in rehab. You shouldn't trust anything she says."

Why would Madeline lie about talking with the CIA? Of course, if she had parlayed with them, why was Ryker here?

"Drugs?" Bishop asked.

"She was on coke the entire time she was talking to me. So, what's your role in all this? Our beautiful Kat mentioned something about another Mr. West," Ryker said. Switching back to his British accent, he said, "Have you been pretending to be me, Scott?"

Bishop couldn't explain everything about the op to surveil Greyson and how it turned into an undercover assignment, so he took a different tack. "We have a mutual friend. General Davis."

Ryker visibly relaxed. "You're one of Davis's boys?"

Bishop nodded but didn't lower his weapon.

Ryker slid his gun back into his jacket and stepped over to Greyson's office door. He looked inside. "Greyson's dead. Little Miss Silencer put two in the chest and one in the head. We need to get out of the building."

"This is a crime scene," Bishop said. "We're not going anywhere."

Ryker laughed again. "I'm not sitting in lock-up for another day and a half while the local LEOs sort out your creds and burn me. Unless you're carrying ID that will get us past the cops, then I'm out."

Ryker was right. Bishop wasn't FBI Special Agent Scott Bishop right now, he was Ryker West. Unfortunately, so was the man in front of him.

"Fuck," Bishop said, lowering his gun.

"Yes, they both have guns," Bishop heard Kat say.

Bishop took the phone from Kat and hung it up.

Ryker pointed at Kat. "Can she be trusted?"

"Can I be trusted?" Kat said. "You're the ones with fake accents and guns."

"And you're still alive," Ryker said. "Count your blessings."

"Security will be here any minute," Kat said, then muttered, "elevators willing."

Bishop eyed Ryker. "She's mine. I'll handle it."

Kat gave Bishop an annoyed look.

Ryker chuckled. "Does she know that?"

Thankfully, Kat didn't say anything.

"Well, your girl is in this knee deep," Ryker said. "Ask her about the murders at the bistro. Ask her why the Dragon is trying to kill her. Ask her why the Dragon just killed her boss." Looking at Kat, he said, "Where are the stairs?"

Kat pointed down the hall, away from the elevators.

What did Ryker mean? Was Kat at the bistro yesterday? "What are you talking about?" Bishop said.

Ryker took a pen from Kat's desk. "Ask your girl."

Bishop looked at Kat.

"Long story," she said.

"We'll talk about this later," Bishop said to Kat, then focused on Ryker. "How do you know the shooter? I didn't get a good look at her." Not that Bishop knew what the Dragon looked like.

Ryker scrawled something on a business card, dropped the pen back on Kat's desk, then tucked the card in Bishop's jacket pocket. "I spotted the Dragon at Byron's Bistro yesterday. She was in the crowd. Your girl was the only one to walk away. I didn't put it together until now. How that connects to this," he said, pointing to Greyson's office, "I don't know—yet. But you and I both know the local police can't help. Stay if you want, but I'm out."

Without another word, Ryker took off in the direction Kat indicated. He didn't wait for Bishop to follow.

"What does he mean?" Kat asked. "Why would someone be trying to kill me? The bistro yesterday was wrong place, wrong time. No one knew I was going there. And why would that same person want to kill Mr. Greyson?"

Tears welled in Kat's eyes. Did she have some feelings for her boss? *Not the right time, Scott.*

"The police are here to discuss a murder you witnessed. Someone named Smith," Bishop said. "Was that at Byron's yesterday?"

"First, I didn't witness a murder. That Smith guy was at Byron's Saturday night but I never met him. Second, I lost my earring. That's why I was at the bistro yesterday. I wasn't looking for you, if that's what you were thinking."

Bishop tried not to look offended. He could tell Kat was rattled. He holstered his gun. "Just explain what happened. Did the Dragon try to kill you yesterday?"

"I was shot—grazed really—it's nothing. The staff was killed—the surveillance tapes were wiped. Like I said, I was there to find my earring. I wasn't supposed to be there," Kat said. "There's no way the shooter was there to kill me."

"No, it sounds like she was there to destroy evidence," he said. "She could have been there Saturday night." Bishop took out his phone. He had to contact Madeline. "Maybe the Dragon's the last one to see Smith alive. Of course, that doesn't explain why the police are here to talk to you."

Bishop opened his texting app. Madeline was either incompetent or her communication skills were reckless. She or Jerry should be monitoring the local news. At the very least she should have texted him about the murders at Byron's.

BISHOP: The Dragon just killed Greyson. She also shot up
Byron's Bistro yesterday, and may be connected to
another murder from Saturday night. What the fuck is

going on, Madeline? Why aren't you on top of this? Call me

Bishop was also pissed about her handling of Ryker. Madeline should have notified him the minute Ryker was released into CIA custody. This disregard for protocol was unacceptable. Bishop needed to talk to Reece, but first he had to get the hell out of this building before security or the cops arrived.

"Smith died the night we had dinner," Kat said, wringing her hands.

"Yeah, it sounds like it," Bishop said. "Now we need to go."

Kat wasn't listening to him.

"I think he was supposed to be my blind date," she said. "And he looked like you—sort of, with a beard. Oh—not like you. He looked like the real West. You were pretending to be West, but Smith had the beard."

Bishop wasn't sure where Kat was going with this.

"Don't you see," she said. "Don't you understand what this means?"

"Not exactly," Bishop said, "but we need to go."

Bishop reached out to take Kat's arm, but she pulled away.

"The police are here to talk to me, because they think I'm her. They saw her on the tapes with Smith." Kat looked at Bishop. "I can't do this. This is like some weird version of *Vertigo*, only I'm not dead yet."

None of this was making sense. "Her who?" Kat couldn't be talking about the Dragon.

"The dragon chick. Aren't you keeping up? Everyone looks like everyone else. I saw her at Byron's Saturday night. She looked like me. I'm going to need an alibi."

Bishop ran his hand through his hair. He didn't like all the parallels, but staying here and hashing it out now wasn't going to work. "I don't have my credentials on me, but when I get them, we'll straighten out this situation with the cops." Bishop held out his hand to Kat. "We need to go. If you need an alibi, I can't do that right now. I also don't like coincidences. You being shot at twice in two days, and now your boss dead, isn't normal. Ryker ID'ing the Dragon puts this in a whole different ballgame." Bishop had to get control of the situation and he couldn't do that here. "We can't get tied up with the locals. Everything about this case is insane. You have to come with me. We have to get this information to the FBI."

"No. I'm not going anywhere with you," Kat said, pushing to her feet. "You thought I was a hooker."

Bishop wasn't about to let Kat out of his sight. "I'm sorry about that. Technically, Ryker West thought you were a hooker. Okay, that doesn't make sense. I'll explain it on the way to the safe house."

He wanted her protected, then he'd sort out everything with the cops. He also needed to let Ryker know that Jayda may have tried to kill him once already. Fuck.

"No," she said.

Bishop smiled. "You're cute when you're angry, but this is non-negotiable."

Bishop heard the ding of the elevator. Without giving her time to call out, he scooped her up like a sack of potatoes and ran for the stairs.

25

KAT

Kat wasn't sure if she should laugh or cry. West—or FBI Special Agent Scott Bishop, if he was to be believed—just threw her over his shoulder like a damn damsel in distress.

"Put me down, jackass," she yelled, trying to kick herself loose.

They were in the stairwell before he responded.

"No. We have to get out of the building before either of us is arrested," Bishop said.

"What? Stop, stop. Put me down. I can walk," she said, pushing against his shoulder.

At the next landing he put her on her feet. Kat could hear footsteps running, which was probably the other Mr. West.

Bishop grabbed her hand to pull her down the stairs.

"No," she said, jerking her hand back. "Not until you show me some ID."

He sighed. "I'm FBI Special Agent Scott Bishop, but I've been undercover as Ryker West for the last few days. I don't have any official ID on me. We need to get out of this building before they find Greyson's body and shut the whole block down."

Kat crossed her arms over her chest. "You have to have some ID."

Bishop ran his hand through his hair. She thought he was super sexy when he did that—now wasn't the time.

"I have ID at the safe house," he said. "We need to go. We can talk once we get to safety."

"So, you've been undercover as the Mr. West guy that came to the office today?" Kat asked, not quite believing what was happening. "The same guy that looks like the dead Mr. Smith. This is crazy. This. Is. Crazy."

Bishop held out his hand. "Not arguing that point, but we can't get stuck with the cops. The FBI needs this information before the Dragon skips town."

Bishop sounded sincere, but everything about the last three days was insane. Kat glanced back toward the seventh-floor door. What if he was right? What if this dragon chick disappeared before they could get word to the FBI? What if she then came back to take care of witnesses? Kat reluctantly took his hand. So far at least he'd not tried to kill her. At some point that had to stop being her go to rationale for trust. Not today, of course.

"I'm not a hooker," she said as they crossed the third-floor landing. "Or escort, or whatever you thought I was."

"I heard you mention that upstairs," Bishop said.

"I just wanted to make sure."

"I did, and I'm glad you're not an escort," he said.

"And why were you—Ryker—meeting an escort anyway?"

"She was a welcome gift from Greyson."

"What? That's not true. Mr. Greyson sells high-end real estate. He's not a pimp."

"He sold high end real estate to a lot of foreign clients with questionable funds," Bishop said as they reached the ground floor.

Was her boss really the guy Bishop was describing?

"This way," Kat said. "We can go out through the service entrance."

Bishop tugged against her hand to stop her. "What's the other way?"

"Lobby, security, and at this point probably cops."

Kat held her purse strap with one hand. Luckily, she'd had it with her in the bathroom. She could bolt as soon as they were outside.

"You look jumpy," he said.

Kat narrowed her eyes. Was he really going there?

"People keep shooting at me," Kat said. "And I'm with a guy that was pretending to be the guy that looks like a guy that got killed by a woman that looked like me that then came and killed my boss, so yeah, I'm a little jumpy," Kat said, trying not to look like she was considering running away at her first opportunity.

"I know you don't want to trust me, but you need to. I don't trust that Jayda Dragon won't come back to kill you. She's tried at least twice," he said.

"The first time was a fluke. I think. Hell, I don't know. But why am I being targeted?"

"I don't like coincidences," Bishop said. "We'll get you safe, and I'll go back to the FBI. Then we'll figure everything out. I promise."

Kat wanted to believe him, and not because he'd been the best one-night stand of her life. She hadn't wanted to be so wrong about someone as she'd thought she was about West—Bishop. That was why she'd freaked about the money. She couldn't believe she'd read the situation so badly, but maybe she hadn't. Maybe he was a nice guy that was pretending to be someone that would sleep with an escort. Actually, he had slept with who he thought was an escort, so what did that say about him?

"I want proof of your identity before I go into anything you're calling a safe house," Kat said, putting air quotes around safe house.

Bishop nodded. "Fair enough, but first we have to get out of this building."

"It really is this way, but there is a maintenance office we'll have to pass. They may be on the lookout. Smokers use this exit, so we may not get stopped, but be ready."

"Lead the way," Bishop said.

26

JAYDA

Jayda's phone buzzed. It was Ana. This job was seriously starting to piss her off. She'd had to kill a security guard just to get out of the building. Now Ana Fucking Ivanov was calling her as she was trying to calmly leave the area.

"Yes, what do you want?" Jayda asked.

"That is no way to speak with your superior," Ana chided.

Jayda wished she was at the hotel with Ana now. She'd make her death a masterpiece. She considered hailing a taxi, but there was no time for that distraction. Ana's death would have to wait.

"Sorry, your highness. How may I help you?" Jayda asked.

"I got the text for Greyson. I thought we'd discussed a murder/suicide."

Was she serious? Jayda never agreed to a staged death scene. "I don't do gimmicks."

"Go back and handle it. Use Greyson's secretary, or that imbecile that sits in the seventh-floor lobby."

Jayda was about to tell Ana where to shove it, when she thought of a better plan. "I have another idea. It will solve a problem for me and deflect Greyson's murder onto his assistant. Get me her home address and I'll handle it."

It was perfect. Jayda would go to Kat's apartment, kill her roommate, wait for Kat to return and kill her, too. Assuming all the stars aligned, Ana would get her murder/suicide after all, just with a twist. Jayda would have Kat write a confession about killing her boss, her roommate, and maybe Smith—before, of course, shooting herself—that would keep Jayda out of the investigation into Smith and deflect attention to the secretary in the Greyson case. Perhaps she could get Madeline onboard to help sell the narrative. Jayda could threaten Madeline with exposure otherwise.

There was also the issue of the agent. Jayda knew Madeline was running an op against Greyson, but she had no reason to suspect Ana. Continuing her ruse as Ana, Jayda would ask Madeline to deflect suspicion away from the real shooter. Simple.

"Why would I help you?" Ana asked.

"If you don't, I'll send all of Greyson and Koshy's private files to the FBI. The files implicate you," Jayda said.

"In what way?"

Jayda didn't actually have any files, but Ana didn't need to know that. "Every way. They have dates and amounts. Every illegal dollar that was funneled to you. It's all documented."

"You fucking bitch. I should have never hired you," Ana yelled.

"Just get me the address and you no longer have to worry about me." That was a total lie. Jayda still planned to kill Ana.

"What makes you think I have the information?" Ana asked.

"You have your own login to his accounts. I'm assuming you can do a company look-up, or send an email to HR. I don't fucking care, just get me the address. Or I go to the FBI. You have fifteen minutes."

Jayda was over this entire fucked up job. She would never work for another Ivanov again. She had to become invisible. The cops would be looking for a girl with pink hair. In the hotel it hadn't looked so pronounced, but in the daylight what she thought had started to look more blonde was now a screaming neon pink.

Spotting a drugstore, Jayda ducked inside to get new hair dye. She had to do something bold. Maybe she would go black. It would be hell to grow out but at this point what choice did she have.

Jayda's phone buzzed while she was in line to pay for the hair dye. It was Ana. She'd found the girl's address. Finally, something was going right. Jayda grabbed an NYC souvenir hat by the register.

"This, too," she said to the cashier.

Jayda shoved her hair inside the cap then hailed a taxi.

27

BISHOP

Bishop and Kat didn't stop walking until they were a block and a half away from her office. Taking out his phone, he opened Uber. Bishop typed in an address near the FBI safe house and summoned a driver. Within minutes they were picked up and on their way to the location where Madeline had been holding Ryker until he could be transported to Texas. Obviously that transport never happened. Madeline better have answers this time, or Bishop was going directly to Reece.

He considered texting Madeline, but she'd been ignoring his texts. Calling was out of the question. He couldn't risk Kat or the Uber driver hearing their conversation. If Madeline wasn't at the safe house for his debrief, he'd call her from there.

Bishop didn't appreciate the way Madeline was running the op. She should have informed him about the shooting at the restaurant. Ignorance of the event was also unacceptable. The entire assignment had been one unexpected change after another. First it was surveillance only, then it was an undercover mission, and now it was a CIA-connected murder investigation.

Bishop just wanted a concise discussion about the state of the case. He refused to be kept in the dark any longer.

Bishop felt a rhythmic motion against his leg. Kat's right leg was bouncing up and down as if she had caffeine jitters, and she was clutching her purse as if a mugger was about to snatch it away.

"Are you okay?" Bishop asked.

Kat glanced at the driver. "I will be. So, what's the long story about the hooker?"

Bishop noticed the driver straighten in his seat.

"Let's talk about that at the—house," Bishop said, not wanting to give the driver any more juicy gossip. He'd also like to avoid discussing the details of Ryker's call girl specs. "I'm going to have a friend look into the issue with the local cops. I'd like to have more details before I contact them. Plus, he might find a connection to Jayda. How exactly did you meet her?"

"I wouldn't say I met her. She was coming out of the restroom and shoulder checked me."

"On purpose?"

"I don't think so, but it was why I noticed her. She was wearing the same dress as me, with obviously fake red hair, but I wouldn't have seen her without the collision."

"How did you know the hair was fake?" Bishop asked.

Kat gave him a questioning look. "Seriously?"

Bishop wasn't sure what she meant. "The hair. How did you know it wasn't natural?"

Kat laughed.

"What's so funny?"

"It was really red. Like impossibly red. Seriously, you've never noticed fake red hair? Ohmygod," Kat laughed harder. "That's why it was pink today!"

Bishop had noticed the shooter's hair was pink, but hadn't given it a lot of thought. He still wasn't clear how it could go from fake red Saturday to pink on Monday. Before he could ask, Kat explained.

"The color was temporary. Her natural hair must be really

light. When you wash out temp color, it can stain your natural hair. So the fake red made pink. Which means the police aren't going to match the pink-haired assassin to the Saturday footage. I'm screwed. They'll think I'm her."

"Don't make assumptions," Bishop said. "Unless the footage is so poor it wouldn't hold up in court, they have to know there were two identical women on the tapes. And if the quality is good, they can do facial recognition to match the women from Saturday to the assassin today. Hair color won't affect that match."

"Okay, so it's possible the police can link Jayda to the tapes from Saturday?"

"Yes."

"But if they don't think I'm connected to Smith—because they see two women on the tapes—what other reason would they have to talk to me?" Kat asked.

Bishop wanted to surround Kat with protective bubble wrap and tell her not to worry, but smothering her wasn't what she needed. He was sure the police had been able to identify two separate women on the tapes, but even if they hadn't they couldn't tie Kat to the incident anyway. But he could tell she was worried. A bunch of maybes weren't going to help. "You physically ran into your double? If they saw that, it's possible they want you to review mugshots or provide an eyewitness account of events."

Kat was biting her thumbnail and looking out the window deep in thought. "Maybe."

Bishop brought up his texting app and clicked on Alex's last chat.

> BISHOP: See what you can find out about a body found in New Jersey yesterday. Last name Smith. Somehow connected to Byron's Bistro
> BISHOP: BTW, Jayda Dragon is in play. She killed Greyson and probably Smith. Inform Meghan

BISHOP: Kaitlyn Fox is with me (she was my date Saturday night—long story)
BISHOP: Ryker West (guy in pic/CIA) is no longer in FBI custody. He says CIA knows nothing about the op
BISHOP: Headed to the safe house now.Madeline isn't returning texts. Have Meghan check with Tyson—did Madeline contact him about the Ivanov connection to Greyson?

Bishop put away his mobile. Alex hadn't immediately responded, but Bishop did just blow up his phone with research requests. He'd check back in with his friend when he got to the safe house.

Leaning back into the seat, Bishop looked over at Kat. He couldn't believe he was sitting here beside her. When she left the hotel yesterday morning, he assumed he'd never see her again. Now she was with him, and not as the escort he'd thought she was. Fuck. He'd treated her like a call girl. He'd had crazy mind-blowing sex with her, then paid her $3,000. No wonder she was being cold toward him. He'd loved the girl next door vibe he got off her, but at the end of the day he knew—or thought he knew—what he was dealing with. It was finally hitting him that although she was weirdly involved in all of this stuff with Ryker and Greyson she wasn't an escort.

From her perspective, he'd been a complete dick.

Bishop wanted to make it up to her, but he didn't know what to do. Should he apologize or reintroduce himself and start over?

Thrusting out his hand, he said, "Hi, my name's Scott. You come here often?"

Kat looked at his hand but didn't take it. Raising an eyebrow, she gave him an *is-that-the-best-you've-got* look.

Bishop raised his hands in surrender. "Okay, okay. I see I'm going to have to kick it up a notch. Here's an oldie but a goodie—

straight out of middle school—it's a good thing I have my library card, because I'm totally checking you out."

Kat's lip turned up in a half smile for a second, then she schooled her features.

"Alright, I see you're going to be a tough sell, but I've got this." Bishop cleared his throat. "Are you a parking ticket? Because you've got *fine* written all over you."

Bishop heard the driver chuckle. He ignored him. Kat was trying to hold back a smile.

Giving Kat his best serious look, he said, "Do you believe in love at first sight—or should I walk by again?"

Kat laughed. She had a beautiful laugh.

"Wow, Mr. Sexy, you sure do know how to smooth talk the ladies," Kat said.

Bishop remembered something Kat said about Smith. "You said Smith was supposed to be your date? What did you mean?"

Kat shrugged and shook her head. "I signed up for a dating service. NYC Blind Date. Apparently, Smith was Gandalf-22."

Bishop chuckled. "That's why you asked about Lord of the Rings, and you called me Gandalf at one point, too. I had no clue what you meant. I thought it was just the lethal martini talking."

"Oh, yeah, that martini was potent. And now I understand why you said Game of Thrones. I knew I wasn't wrong. I had gotten it right. You just weren't Gandalf."

Bishop was finally getting Kat to open up. Without thinking he grabbed her hand to hold it. She gave a slight tug but didn't try very hard to get him to release it.

"I don't think you realize how glad I am that you aren't what I thought you were." Bishop glanced at the driver who was doing a horrible job of pretending not to listen.

"Yeah, me too," Kat said, squeezing his hand.

The car slowed and the driver pulled alongside the curb.

"We're here," the driver said.

Kat exited on her side. Bishop slid across the seat to exit behind her.

"Which way?" Kat asked.

Bishop pointed to the right. "We're close. Just a couple of blocks."

He started to take her hand, then realized how that might look, then decided he didn't care. Kat let him take her hand, which lifted a weight he hadn't realized was there.

Bishop's phone buzzed. It was a text from an unknown number.

UNKNOWN: Safe house compromised. Lose this phone. Go to Valhalla

28

KAT

Kat had started to relax, which was weird considering all the shit that was actively happening around her. Maybe it was Bishop—did he make her feel safe in life threatening situations?—or maybe it was just the lull in all the excitement. They'd made it out of the building, no one was currently shooting at them, and Mr. Sexy seemed happy she wasn't a hooker. At this point she was ready to take a win where she could get it.

And now he was holding her hand. She liked the feeling of being linked to him. It felt comfortable. It felt right.

Bishop got a text. His demeanor changed as he read it. He went from casual, let's-get-to-the-safe-house-so-we-can-talk to high alert special agent in charge.

"Change of plans," he said. "We can't stay here."

Bishop scanned the area.

"What are you looking for?" Kat asked.

Bishop guided her toward the intersection.

"I thought you said the safe house was back there," Kat said.

"It's not safe. It's been compromised," Bishop said.

Had Kat made the wrong decision to trust Bishop? Was this all just a ruse? Did he really get her away from her office and the cops to protect her? Or was he trying to protect himself?

Breathe, Kat thought. Her adrenaline had been running hot for days. She needed to think this through. At the office, everyone had been shot at. Greyson had been killed by the assassin, Jayda. All three of them had seen Jayda come out of Greyson's office carrying a gun. She was obviously the killer.

Bishop was pretending to be West, and the real West was there too, but what could she have done to either of them if she'd stayed at the office and talked to the cops? Nothing. They weren't the killers and according to Bishop he was FBI, which meant he could have cleared his name. Unless Ryker had been in the country illegally, or he'd committed a crime on US soil, the cops would have nothing on him. Even if Bishop was lying or Ryker was wanted for another crime, Kat couldn't have given the cops anything on them. The building had security cameras at the entrance. She wouldn't even have needed to give a description.

That meant Bishop could have walked away just like Ryker. He could have left her there to talk with the cops, but he didn't. He must truly believe she was in danger.

Maybe Kat was being naïve, but she had to believe he didn't have ill intent. Cheesy pick-up lines, yes, ill intent, no. Her danger-meter was off the charts with him, but she still felt safe. He made her feel protected.

"Okay, you say the safe house isn't secure," Kat said. "I'm going to trust you, but please tell me what we're doing."

"We're going to get new phones and get out of town," Bishop said.

The light turned as they reached the intersection. Bishop didn't slow down. He continued to lead her across the street.

Kat's hand was on her bag and she clutched it tighter at the thought of having to give up her phone. "Will they be looking for my phone?"

"Yes. Once the FBI learns of Greyson's death, they'll connect your disappearance to the crime and they'll start looking for you, too."

Kat didn't like where this was going. "But you said the safe house is compromised. Who in the FBI would be investigating? And if they don't know about Greyson's death yet, then how did the safe house get compromised?"

Bishop stopped on the sidewalk in front of an electronics store. He turned to face her. "I don't have the answers yet. We need to get to a safe location, then we'll figure out what went wrong. Okay?"

Kat nodded. She was scared, but trusting Bishop felt right.

"How much money do you have?" Bishop asked. "We need to get out of the city, but first we've got to become invisible."

"I never carry—" Kat laughed.

"What?"

"Today's our lucky day. I have the hooker money. I'd planned to donate it to a no-kill shelter near the office, but I was running late this morning." Kat patted her purse. "I've still got the cash."

Bishop's eyebrows drew together. "That money was requisitioned from the FBI for the op, which means it's traceable."

"It's no good to use? Oh, no, what if I'd given it to the shelter?" Kat asked. "Wait a minute. Were you planning to arrest the escort?"

"Not exactly," Bishop said.

"Which part?"

"The money is traceable, but someone would have to be looking for it. In the case of the escort, the money would have been used as leverage to force the escort to testify against Greyson if she was connected to the case. For our purposes, using the money should be safe. But it is best if we line up a new source soon just in case."

Kat shook her head. "I'm glad now I was running late, but that money would have helped the shelter."

Lifting her chin with his hand, Bishop gave her a light kiss on the lips. She leaned in, letting the kiss linger a moment longer.

Bishop caressed her cheek. "After this is over, I'll make sure the animal shelter gets their donation. In untraceable funds."

Kat smiled, her cheeks blushing. "Thanks." She pulled the envelope out of her purse.

Bishop placed his hand over hers. "Leave it in your bag for now. Just take out $300."

Kat nodded. Tearing open the top of the envelope, she tugged out a few bills, and passed them to Bishop.

"I'll get the phones. You hang back so it doesn't look like we're together. I'm sure this place has cameras, so keep your head down," Bishop said.

"Okay."

Kat followed Bishop into the shop. She kept her head down as she browsed the shelves. Bishop headed to the counter. Using his British accent, he bought two phones with chargers, selecting the unlimited data, text, and talk plan. Activating the phones took longer than expected, but they would be partially charged and ready to use immediately. Kat bought two wireless earbuds before exiting the shop with Bishop.

Once they were on the sidewalk, Bishop held out his hand. "I need your phone."

Kat hesitated. This was her life—sort of. Okay, it was just her way of reaching the outside world—her safety blanket.

"The phone is backed-up right?" he said. "This is just a small inconvenience until we can get this mess sorted out. I'll replace your phone when this is over. I promise."

"You're racking up quite a tally, Mr. Sexy. How exactly are you going to cover your debts?" Kat asked.

"Maybe I can work it off?" he said, with a completely straight face.

Kat couldn't help laughing. "We'll see," she said, reluctantly handing her phone to Bishop.

Kat watched as Bishop pulled apart both phones, removing the SIM cards and batteries. He put the busted phones in the bag from the electronics store, then motioned for her to follow. They walked two blocks before he dumped the contents of the bag into a trash can.

Bishop held up his hand to hail a taxi. "We're getting out of the city."

"We have to get Rip first," Kat said. She wasn't leaving her best friend here to fend for himself.

Bishop shook his head.

"Look, you put me in this situation. I don't know why the assassin tried to kill West and then killed Mr. Greyson. Even if she doesn't know I'm the woman she bumped into at the restaurant, she has to know now that I'm the one she shot at yesterday. And now I've seen her and can tie Mr. Greyson's murder to her. She's also got to know she didn't kill West. I have no idea who hired her, but what if that person is connected to someone at the company? What if that person has access to my home address? Or maybe she was there to steal his hard drive—fuck, maybe she already has my address."

Bishop tried to interrupt her, but Kat held up her hand.

"I get it, you probably think I'm overthinking things, but I'm not willing to risk my friend's wellbeing." She'd been up to her neck in risk lately. She wouldn't roll the dice on Rip's safety. "Rip could be in trouble and I refuse to leave town without him."

"Kat, it isn't—"

"He comes with us, or you can go without me. I will not budge on this."

Bishop sighed. "Okay, but I've got to arrange some things first."

Bishop took out his new phone and started typing.

"What are you doing?"

"I'm adding the unknown number to my contacts. It's from a burner phone Alex used to warn us about the safe house. I'll text

Alex on that number to let him know we need transportation for three," Bishop said.

"Are they going to send a car? Is that dangerous?"

Kat didn't like the uncertainty. She wanted to get Rip and go into hiding until this all blew over.

Bishop was texting, then looked up toward the intersection. Kat looked in the same direction but didn't see anything. Before she could ask the plan, he put his phone away and took her hand.

"Let's go. A buddy of mine is arranging a car for us," Bishop said.

With her hand in his, she followed him. "Should I call Rip?"

"Let's get the car first. If the police are talking to him, I'd prefer he not get a call from our new phones until we have the means to pick him up."

Kat nodded. It sounded like a reasonable plan.

29

JAYDA

Jayda considered texting Madeline to add Ana's new alias to the no-fly list, but Ana may have fixed the typo on the IDs, and if Ana was picked up she could easily turn on Jayda, making it impossible for her to leave the country. Her path was set. She'd take care of the roommate and Kat, then Ana—if Ana was still in the US, otherwise Evgeni would need to finish her off. Everything was getting too complicated. She had to uncomplicate things. For that she needed information. She brought up Madeline's last text.

JAYDA: I need information. What do they have on Greyson's shooter?
FBI_FOOL: Not a good time
JAYDA: Make time, or things will not end well for you
FBI_FOOL: Don't threaten me. What do you care anyway? You said this had nothing to do with you
JAYDA: He was a business associate and friend. I would like to pay my respects to the family by bringing them the head of his killer
FBI_FOOL: I can't let you do that

JAYDA: You do not let me do anything

Fuck, Jayda had to chill. Madeline was a fool, but she was still part of the FBI. Of course, Jayda was pretending to be Ana, so fuck the consequences. Jayda continued.

JAYDA: I will have my revenge
FBI_FOOL: I can't just stop an investigation. The shooter is on film. There is an APB out for her arrest. Her image will be on every evening news cast
JAYDA: You need to stall them—tell them you have a lead, but you can't spook the shooter by releasing the photo to the media
FBI_FOOL: That may not be possible
JAYDA: Then I can't guarantee your protection

Jayda waited as Madeline typed. If Madeline couldn't get this stopped, she'd have to abandon her plan to kill Kat and leave right now. Madeline responded.

FBI_FOOL: I can get you twenty-four hours, but I need a favor
JAYDA: What favor?
FBI_FOOL: Elimination of target: Scott Bishop, FBI, NYC…picture attached

Jayda looked at the picture. It was the agent that had met with Greyson. Why would Madeline want him dead? Jayda was about to ask when Madeline texted.

FBI_FOOL: He's currently in the wind. Traveling with Kaitlyn Fox

Jayda couldn't believe it. Madeline wanted one of her agents dead and that agent was with Kat.

> JAYDA: Your agent is with Greyson's assistant?
> FBI_FOOL: Yes
> JAYDA: What should I do with the girl?
> FBI_FOOL: Not my problem, but I need Bishop out of the way and unable to contradict me
> JAYDA: For this, I need you to put a hold on circulating the shooter's image for 48 hours
> JAYDA: I also need his last known whereabouts and any leads you get along the way. And keep the cops away from Kaitlyn's apartment. They may go there
> FBI_FOOL: Affirmative. Notify me when the job is complete

Jayda wanted to do a happy dance but kept her emotions in check. The FBI fool would help her find the secretary. It was kismet.

The taxi dropped off Jayda at Kat's apartment. Jayda considered leaving the roommate out of it and just wait for Madeline to give her a lead. But that could take hours and Jayda still needed to dye her hair. Plus, it wouldn't hurt to have leverage. The roommate would make it easier for Jayda to lure Kat out into the open if Kat had already gone to ground.

Putting on her most pleasant smile, Jayda knocked on Kat's door.

"Delivery," she said.

After a few seconds she knocked again. The roommate must not be home. Jayda took out her lock picks and made fast work of getting into the apartment.

Jayda closed and locked the door behind her. She surveyed the room. The apartment wasn't very big, but New York City apartments never were. Jayda checked the bedrooms. Both were clear.

She began to look around, then remembered the hair dye. Checking Kat's closet, she grabbed a purple Pride March T-shirt and cargo pants. Jayda felt a younger look would help her blend in. She went into the bathroom to change clothes and apply the permanent color to her hair. Processing would take twenty minutes. Once the gloppy mixture saturated her hair, she set the timer on her phone.

To kill the time, Jayda decided to search the apartment. She started her search in Rip's room. Unlike Kaitlyn's room, which had been messy and looked lived in, Rip's room was excessively neat and tidy. Jayda found a Christmas card and pride rainbow pin stuck to his corkboard. The envelope was tucked behind the picture card, which showed an older couple. The note read: "Love Mom and Dad."

Jayda snapped a photo of his parents' picture and the address on the envelope and texted those to Evgeni.

JAYDA: Keep this for insurance. If I don't check in every hour, have someone kill them

Typing bubbles appeared almost immediately. Evgeni texted back.

EVGENI: What happened?
JAYDA: I'll explain later. I'll need new IDs
EVGENI: Where's Ana?
JAYDA: Still alive, side mission will have to wait
EVGENI: We must talk
JAYDA: Later, I have to tie up loose ends first
EVGENI: I'll need new pictures for IDs
JAYDA: Working on that now. Will be in touch soon

Jayda put away her phone. She searched Kat's room next. Jayda was surprised when she found a calendar tacked above Kat's desk

—did no one use Google calendars to track their events? Saturday's square had the word *Gandalf-22*. Jayda remembered reading in the newspaper that the guy she killed had a tattoo of Gandalf and his wallet had that ridiculous wizard patch. Smith must have been her date. Instead she got West and Jayda got Smith.

Looking around for more insight, Jayda found a brochure for NYC Blind Dating service. Someone had scrawled Gandalf-22 on the front side. Well, one mystery solved. Smith was there for a blind date with Kat. There was no mutual friend to tie them together.

If the police knew of the dating service, they'd need a warrant to pull Kat's records. Jayda snapped a picture of the brochure and texted it to Evgeni.

JAYDA: Send this to the New Jersey police—it connects Kat with the body
EVGENI: ??
JAYDA: I'll explain later

Jayda's phone timer dinged. She pressed the stop button and went to wash her hair. She was toweling it dry when she heard the door open and close. She remained still, trying not to make any noise.

A male voice said, "Kit Kat, are you here?"

It must be the roommate. Jayda readied her gun and waited for Rip to speak again.

"Kat, are you here?"

The voice was right outside the door. She reached down and unlocked the door, then turned the handle to release the catch. Holding her gun out, she kicked the door as hard as she could. A loud thwack and crash sounded.

"For fuck's sake, Kat," Rip said.

Jayda came out of the bathroom with her gun aimed straight at Rip. He was laying dazed on the floor, holding his bleeding nose.

His eyes widened when he caught sight of the stranger in his apartment. Jayda shot a round into the floor, between his legs, which caused him to try and scoot back.

"Who the fuck are you?" Rip yelled.

"Your worst nightmare, baby," Jayda said.

"Is everything okay in there?" an elderly voice asked from outside in the hall.

Jayda aimed her gun at the door.

"No," Rip pleaded with Jayda, then yelled, "Everything's fine, Miss Rose."

"Okay," Miss Rose said, before shuffling down the hall.

Jayda couldn't stay here. The walls were too thin.

"We're going to take a ride. And before you decide to be a hero, you should know that I've sent your parents' address and photo to a friend of mine. He'll kill them if I don't check in regularly," Jayda said.

Rip swallowed. "Okay."

Jayda tossed him a heavy-duty zip tie. "Put that on. Around your wrists."

Rip did as he was told.

Jayda finger-combed her hair then snapped a quick selfie, using the white wall of the apartment as her backdrop. She sent the photo to Evgeni to use for her new IDs, then leveled her gun at Rip.

"Get up," she said, making sure she could deliver a kill shot if needed. She saw the outline of a phone in his pocket. "Give me your phone. Unlock it first."

Rip removed his phone, unlocked it, and tossed it to her. Jayda found Kat's number and typed out a quick text. It immediately showed as delivered. Jayda tossed Rip's phone into his room. He wouldn't be needing it.

"Wipe the blood off your hands and face, then leave a note for your roommate," Jayda said.

She told Rip what to write, which he left on a small whiteboard on the refrigerator. She handed him her bag to carry, which covered the zip ties keeping his hands together, and summoned an Uber.

"Why are you doing this?" Rip asked. "Why do you want Kat?"

Jayda caressed the side of Rip's cheek. "She was just at the wrong place at the wrong time, and she makes a nice patsy. If you don't cause any trouble you can walk away," Jayda lied.

"Yeah, right," Rip said, jerking his head away from her hand.

Jayda had the Uber driver drop them off at a warehouse in New Jersey. Not the one she'd used Saturday night. This one belonged to Koshy. It wasn't occupied and had no scheduled maintenance. She would be safe here, until she killed Kat and Bishop. Evgeni would have her new IDs ready in a day or two, then she'd leave the US for good.

30

BISHOP

Bishop led Kat to a parking garage where Vincent kept one of his cars. After punching in the code, a lock box opened, presenting Bishop with two key fobs. One fob opened the garage entrance, the other started the Land Rover SUV parked in Vincent's spot.

"What does your friend do exactly?" Kat asked, as they got settled in the vehicle.

Bishop chuckled. "For the last two years he's been finding himself, by living off the land. Before that he was one hell of an Army Ranger, and before that he was a blue blood with a medical degree. You know, the usual."

Kat gave him a strange look, as if she couldn't tell whether he was joking.

Bishop held up three fingers. "Scout's honor."

Kat shook her head. "Does this friend have a name?"

"Vincent York."

"The Vincent York?"

Bishop pressed the ignition and started the car. "The one and only."

Bishop put Kat's address into the nav system.

A ding sounded. Kat raised her wrist.

"Is that an Apple Watch?" Bishop asked. "You can't keep it."

Clearly Kat had never needed to go off the grid. He should have noticed the watch, but he'd never had one. It wasn't something he noticed.

"Ohmygod," Kat said, her hand to her mouth. "No, no, no."

"What is it?" Bishop asked.

"We have to get to the apartment. Jayda has Rip."

Bishop hadn't seriously worried about Rip's safety, and it wasn't because he didn't care. He had no ill will toward the man he'd initial thought was her pimp. He hadn't worried because Kat and Rip lived in a city of millions. How was Jayda supposed to find their apartment? The odds weren't in her favor, and based on the sequence of events, there was no way Jayda knew Kat was Greyson's assistant until after Jayda killed Greyson. That meant Jayda wouldn't have had any reason to take Kat's personal info from Greyson's office. So how the hell had Jayda found Kat's apartment?

"What does the message say?" Bishop asked.

"Rip is such a cutie. I love the apartment. XOXO Jayda," Kat said. "Bishop, we have to help him. She could kill him."

Bishop could hear the fear in Kat's voice. He didn't like seeing her in pain. Reaching over, he took Kat's hand. "We'll save him."

They were outside Kat's apartment within minutes. Kat was out of the car as soon as they parked.

"Hold up," Bishop said, running to catch up.

"We have to help him," Kat said.

"We have to not die while helping him."

Kat stopped. She turned to face him, tears in her eyes. "I can't lose him."

Bishop pulled Kat in for a hug. "Shhh. I just want us to be cautious. No rushing in half-cocked."

"Okay," she said, pulling away from his hold. "I'll follow your lead."

Bishop had his gun out as they approached Kat's door. He could tell before touching it that the door was ajar. He held his left hand up, fist closed. He stopped. Kat bumped into him. He put his finger to his lips to remind her to be quiet. Holding his hand out flat toward her, he made a pushing motion. Hopefully she'd know that meant to stay put.

Bishop listened. He didn't hear anything, but he also wasn't convinced Jayda wasn't lying in wait. He pushed the door open, just as an elderly woman exited her apartment.

Bishop quickly tucked his gun behind his back.

"Kaitlyn," the woman said, causing Kat to jump. "What are you doing out here?"

Kat rushed over to the older woman. "Shhhh, it's a surprise," Kat whispered.

"Now, child, you know I can't hear when you talk like that. I'm glad to see Rip has finally found himself a girl."

Bishop froze. He gave Kat a nod toward the elderly lady.

"Miss Rose, who do you mean? Kat asked.

"That dark haired girl that he left with. She was awfully pretty," Miss Rose said.

Kat just smiled.

Bishop motioned toward the apartment, then continued inside. The place was clear. He heard Kat end her conversation with Miss Rose before she followed him inside.

"Did she see anything else?" Bishop asked, as he scanned the living room for clues.

"She said the woman had black hair, but that's it," Kat said.

"Do a quick search—see if anything is missing or out of place. We can't stay here long, and you need to leave your watch when we go."

"What if she texts again?" Kat said.

"Can you text from that thing?" Bishop asked, pointing at the watch.

"Yes."

"Try contacting him."

Kat pressed a button then said, "Rip, are you okay?" She pressed another button. Almost immediately a chirp sounded from a bedroom in the back. "That's his phone," she said.

Kat retrieved Rip's cellphone from his bedroom.

"Look around. There has to be something here that will lead us to finding them," Bishop said.

Not knowing where to look, he did a cursory search of the entire apartment. The bathroom reeked of chemicals. He spotted a box of black hair dye in the trash, and there were two towels on the floor covered in the remnants of grayish-black dye. There was a mess around the sink, and lots of debris on the floor.

"Nothing looks out of place," Kat said.

"Okay. Pack an overnight bag. We have to get out of here."

Kat looked at the mess in the bathroom.

"It'll be okay," he said.

Kat nodded, then returned to her bedroom.

Bishop wanted to know how Jayda got Kat's address. She'd worked for the Ivanovs before and had ties to Evgeni Petrov, the assassin that shot Haden. Could she have gotten the address from Ana? Ana had ties to Greyson. Was Ana the one who hired Jayda to kill Greyson?

Bishop took out his burner phone and brought up Alex's anonymous contact info that he'd named Ranger 8. Alex still hadn't replied to all his texts from earlier. Bishop needed to know what they'd found out.

BISHOP: Question: could Ana have hired Jayda to take out Greyson?
RANGER8: Hold on

A minute later his phone rang. It was the unknown number.

"What have you heard?" Bishop asked.

"I can't talk long," Alex said. Bishop could hear the sound of wind in the background. Alex had left FBI Headquarters. "You are in a shit ton of trouble, bro."

"I get that, but why? What is happening? Why was the safe house compromised?"

"Your field supervisor is accusing you of killing Special Agent Jerry Osborn."

Fucking hell, Jerry was dead? And Madeline was trying to pin it on him.

Alex continued, "There's an APB out for your arrest. I could go to jail for talking to you."

What the hell was Madeline up to? "Where was Agent Osborn killed?"

"At the safe house."

"Did they check the surveillance? I haven't been to the safe house yet. What evidence could they have?" Bishop asked.

"Cameras were offline for maintenance. Ryker escaped—they aren't calling him CIA. The evidence they have is super-secret. No one knows, not even Tyson."

Ryker was connected to General Davis, which might explain the cloak and dagger handling, but it didn't explain why they wouldn't have him officially tied to the CIA or to an agency that was redacted.

"This is crazy," Bishop said. "Jerry was a newbie. What reason could I possibly have for killing him? And why wouldn't they suspect Ryker?"

Bishop didn't actually believe Ryker had killed Jerry, but Madeline would have had an easier time framing him. And why were the cameras offline? The maintenance answer sounds like bullshit.

"No one is sharing evidence. The whole thing is a cluster and I've been asked to go home if I can't keep my nose out of the investigation. I did hear that you and Jerry weren't getting along. They have text messages and Madeline isn't discouraging the efforts to convict you."

"Fuck," Bishop cursed.

"I do know this. Meghan doesn't trust Madeline. She's the reason Meghan left New York."

Bishop ran his hand through his hair. He had to think of the best way out of this. Should he just turn himself in? Madeline was painting a picture of a rogue agent. They might just shoot him on sight. If he were in Chicago it would be different. He could turn himself into Tyson or Wilson. He'd worked with both men for years. They'd believe him enough to do a fair investigation. He knew no one except Madeline and Jerry—who was now dead—in NYC. He'd only ever emailed Reece. He also didn't trust turning himself into the local cops. He was being framed for killing an FBI agent. They might shoot first and ask questions later.

"Does Meghan think I should turn myself in?" Bishop asked.

"I don't know. She hasn't said, but I know she doesn't trust anything Madeline is involved with. Are you at Valhalla yet?"

Bishop couldn't wait to get to Vincent's house. "Not yet. We're headed there next. Kat insisted we get her roommate first, but Jayda beat us here."

"Shit. Does anyone know?" Alex asked.

"I was going to have you tell Meghan, but now I don't know the best strategy. I'd like to know how Jayda found Kat's address and who hired her. I was hoping Meghan could run that down, but I don't want to put her in a bad situation."

"She already suspects I know more than I'm saying," Alex said.

"How?"

"She asked how I knew Greyson was dead—before it was reported on the news."

"Sorry. I don't want you getting in trouble for me. You need to stay out of this."

"Fuck that. I'm not leaving a man behind. I'll be careful, but I'm staying involved," Alex said.

Bishop needed to hang up now. He couldn't be responsible for his friend going to prison.

"I can hear you thinking," Alex said. "Just know that I'm not dropping this, so you can help me help you, or you can be a dick and stop calling."

Bishop let out a sigh. Alex was right. If he cut him off, that didn't mean Alex wouldn't continue to be involved. At least this way Bishop still had an in at the agency. And Alex was a master of hiding in plain sight.

"Okay, but if you need to, you burn me. I won't have you going to jail because you are trying to protect me. Got it?" Bishop asked.

"Got it."

Bishop heard Kat calling from the kitchen. "Bishop, I found a note."

"Hold on a minute," Bishop said to Alex. Bishop headed for the kitchen. "Where is it?" he asked Kat.

"Here, on the whiteboard," she said.

Kat was standing in the kitchen with her hand over her mouth. She was looking at a small square board attached to the door of the refrigerator. The note said, "Hey, babe, hanging out with J at 1240 Carter. See you soon. RIP." He read it off to Alex.

"I'm on it," Alex said, then hung up.

Kat was shaking her head and muttering, "No, no, no."

Bishop pulled her into a hug. He didn't like seeing her upset.

"Shhh…we're going to find him, okay? We're going to figure out who she's getting her information from, and we're going to get him back," Bishop said.

Kat wiped a few stray tears from her cheeks. "You don't understand. He signed it capital R-I-P."

Bishop didn't know the significance. His name was Rip.

"He hates when people write his name like it's initials. This is his handwriting."

Bishop was still missing something.

"He didn't sign his name. He signed 'Rest in Peace'. Do you see, he's basically saying he's already dead."

Bishop held her closer. "Let's not jump to conclusions. Maybe he meant something else? Jayda wouldn't get rid of her leverage. Finish getting your things. Alex will figure out where that address is, and we'll get him."

"Promise?"

"I promise," Bishop said.

"Okay." Kat wiped her eyes. "I'm ready. I just need a few things from the bathroom. And, did you see the bullet hole?"

Bishop shook his head.

"At least there's no blood around it," Kat said, as she pointed out the notch in the floor.

Grabbing a screwdriver from a junk drawer in the kitchen, Bishop dug out the bullet. He took pictures of the slug and forwarded everything he had to Alex.

Kat came out of the bedroom with a duffel and backpack. She'd also changed out of her office suit and put on jeans and a T-shirt with a light jacket.

"Are you okay?" Bishop asked.

"Not really, but I can't shut down. We have to find him."

Bishop gave Kat another hug, kissing her on the top of the head.

"We'll find him. I've got friends that can help."

31

ALEX

Alex was sitting in the tiny cubicle that he'd been assigned at the FBI office in Chicago. He was working off his deferred community service by assisting the FBI with data analysis for suspected bank fraud. He was basically hacking for the FBI. His tasks included finding the real origin of funds from open criminal cases that were marked suspicious or suspect and training a couple of MIT grads on the latest "Dark Web Strategies"—their words, not his.

The assignment wasn't bad, but even if it had sucked he wouldn't complain, because this was where he had met Meghan.

Meghan Malone was a bad ass FBI agent who'd recently transferred from New York City. She was smart, funny, and serious about her career. She was an Army brat—her dad, a native Hawaiian, had been in the military. Her childhood was spent on bases all over the world. She spoke seven languages and had the most amazing dimples. And she was off limits—sort of.

Meghan was his supervisor. He'd gotten her to agree to coffee and lunch a few times. Dinner was a big no, but he was working on that. He didn't want to fuck up her job at the bureau by being too aggressive. At least while he was working here—after he left, all bets were off.

Then this mess with Bishop exploded. Meghan got pulled in because of her connections to NYC. She'd worked there before transferring to Chicago a month ago. Meghan had requested the transfer, but she felt she'd had no choice. Another agent was using destructive tactics to get ahead, and it was working.

Meghan would still be working in NYC if it weren't for her arch-nemesis, Madeline Maxwell.

Maxwell had scooped Meghan's ideas on a high-profile case. She "uncovered" a large money laundering ring—all based on Meghan's research—and then leveraged that to get a promotion and take another case Meghan had been promised.

Being sidelined in favor of Maxwell was the last straw. Staying wasn't an option.

Alex knew he was biased, but he knew Meghan was still the best agent. This was confirmed when NYC ADIC Reece Patterson personally requested she get involved in the Bishop situation. Reece wanted to know what the fuck had really happened. He didn't like where the case was going. Meghan had confided in Alex that she believed Reece no longer trusted Maxwell.

Unfortunately, the case against Bishop appeared fairly solid. Alex read the report and knew it was total bullshit, but no one in NYC knew him and apparently his Chicago buddies weren't in a position to dissuade them.

First, Maxwell had painted Bishop as a subpar agent who constantly bickered with her and the rookie agent Jerry Osborn. She referenced his questionable performance in Chicago that got him "demoted" to her team—which was bullshit. He'd taken a temporary assignment, not a demotion. Maxwell also referenced text messages and arguments she'd personally witnessed between Jerry and Bishop. Of course, those details would have all been dismissed if it weren't for one thing—Jerry was dead.

He had been shot and killed at the safe house. A full autopsy was pending, but the visual inspection indicated a knot on the back of his head. He'd been struck prior to being shot. Maxwell stated that the ballistics indicated the shot came from Bishop's service weapon, but the ballistics report wasn't part of the file. Meghan had requested they be provided.

If Maxwell was trying to frame Bishop, then she was banking on no one doing a deep dive on her report or finding the actual paper trail offline. Meghan, of course, would leave no stone unturned.

There was also money missing from the operating budget. Maxwell indicated that Bishop had signed out the funds without her knowledge, to play the part of Ryker West. Nothing with Bishop's signature existed in the file, but they were already running the serial numbers on the cash hoping to get a hit.

The timing just didn't feel right. Everything was electronic, but there were too many holes, which was why Meghan had dug deeper into the missing paperwork. She was still waiting for confirmation about the ballistics, but she'd found a discrepancy in Maxwell's story about the money.

Meghan discovered that Jerry was the one who had requisitioned the original funds from finance. Madeline then changed her story to acknowledge money was being requested, but that she'd not been informed that it had been approved. Maxwell then attempted to indicate Jerry and Bishop may have been working together to defraud the project and steal money. Meghan could find nothing to corroborate this assertion, but there was also no evidence to disprove it. Not while Bishop was on the run.

Nothing was adding up, but Bishop was a convenient target.

Also, for no apparent reason, Maxwell had put a hold on releasing the video footage of Greyson's shooter, citing a lead she was running down that might be compromised if the images were released to the media. She'd requested forty-eight hours to investigate.

Alex straightened in his seat as Meghan returned to his desk with a fresh coffee. Now he wished he'd said yes when she asked if he wanted one.

"None of this makes sense," Meghan said, picking up where they'd left off. "And why put the hold on the video footage?"

"I agree. At the very least, Maxwell is making suspicious decisions," Alex said.

"Yes, but Reece needs proof, which means this is going to be a long night. You don't have to stay."

"I'm not leaving. Bishop is like a brother to me. I want to see his name cleared."

"Okay, but cases don't always turn out like you hope. We have to review all the evidence objectively. Reece needs a solid lead to follow if we want Bishop to come out of this," Meghan said.

"I understand, but why isn't Maxwell in custody until all this is sorted out?" Alex asked.

"It isn't that simple. Believe it or not, she's respected—by some. She'd have to really fuck something up to be suspended, and she'd have to be videoed holding a gun to Osborn's head to have her arrested without an investigation."

"Can't you at least get her pulled off this investigation? You read the reports. She's biased as hell."

"So are you, Wren. You think Bishop can do no wrong. He's human. He may have fucked up."

Alex didn't believe it. He knew the kind of man Bishop was. There was no way he'd have killed a fellow agent, not without coming away bloody in a to the death style defense. A clean shot to the back of the head wasn't even a remote possibility.

"What about Ryker," Alex asked. "Why don't they suspect him?"

"That is being hushed up at the highest levels. It's best if you don't even mention his name."

"You know he's CIA, right?" Alex asked.

"I know no such thing, and neither do you. Now, why would

Bishop take Kaitlyn?" Meghan asked, but it was more to herself that to Alex.

Cause he's got the hots for her, Alex thought, but didn't say. Instead, he decided to share facts Meghan would have no reason to tie together. "So, I might have a reason, but you can't ask where I got the info."

Meghan looked at him, her expression telling him that he may have just fucked up.

"Or not—I mean, what do I know?"

"Tell me, then I'll decide."

"Decide what?"

"If you need to be arrested for aiding and abetting."

Was she kidding? Alex didn't think she was kidding.

"Spit it out, Wren," Meghan demanded. "Or we can go talk to ADIC Wilson."

Fuck. Okay, he had to handle this delicately. "Before we knew any of this was happening, Bishop texted me. He wanted me to look up a guy named Smith. He was at Byron's Bistro the same night Bishop and Kat were there. He was found dead in New Jersey on Sunday. I think the shooter was Jayda, and I think she thought Smith was Ryker West."

Meghan closed her eyes and took in a long breath, then released it.

"So, you're telling me that Jayda Dragon was brought in to kill Ryker West?"

Alex shrugged. "Maybe."

"Then she killed Greyson?"

"Definitely—we've seen the tapes."

"Why is that connected to Kaitlyn—I'm sorry, Kat?" Meghan asked.

Crap, Alex had screwed up by using her nickname. Oh well, in for a penny. "Maybe, and what do I really know, but maybe Kaitlyn was suspected in that case because Smith was supposed to be her blind date and she wound up with Ryker West instead. But the local police were there to question her—maybe she thought staying with the FBI guy was a better plan?"

Meghan looked up toward the sky and Alex thought she might have been muttering a prayer. After a few minutes, she said, "Kaitlyn and Bishop knew each other from Saturday night at the restaurant?" Meghan shook her head. "Why would Kaitlyn go with a guy she thought was Ryker West, who she thought was a blind date, who then told her he was FBI? Sounds a little TSTL to me, Wren."

"I'm sure it happened differently. Plus, at that point Bishop thought he was going back to the safe house," Alex said.

"A safe house he never made it to. Are you in contact with Bishop? Don't lie to me."

Fuck. What was Alex supposed to say. He didn't want to lie to Meghan, but he couldn't burn Bishop without a solid plan to get him out of this mess. And he'd not yet mentioned the roommate situation. Alex's search was still running. He'd found six possible addresses within a one-hundred-mile radius, and now he was running those addresses through the case files to see if any of them were known or connected to any existing FBI investigation.

Thankfully, he was saved when Meghan's phone rang. She checked the display.

"I have to take this, but we aren't done with this conversation," Meghan said before walking away to take the call.

Dammit, he was royally screwing this up. He pulled up Vincent's contact. His buddy had already done too much, but he needed assistance and Drake was in no condition right now to help.

ALEX: B may need more help—Patrick Redman help
VINCENT: Mission?
ALEX: Rescue, 1 male, early twenties
VINCENT: Situation?
ALEX: Held by assassin, working on address now

VINCENT: 10-4, standby

Alex checked on the results of his search. He'd gotten a hit on one of the New Jersey addresses. It was a business connected to Joseph Koshy—who was dead. Alex did some Googling and found out Koshy had committed suicide. He'd also been a New York City real estate developer like Greyson. Was he somehow connected to the same money laundering Greyson was suspected of?

Alex pulled up the file Koshy's address was found in. A business was also listed, Golden Rose LLC. Alex dug a little deeper and found Golden Rose in a separate file—this time one created by Meghan and last updated by Madeline.

Was this the case where Maxwell stole some of Meghan's research? Koshy had been suspected of laundering money for the Russians. He was definitely in the same business as Greyson, but there wasn't a full investigation. When Koshy died, the case died with him.

Alex checked a few other sources. Golden Rose LLC was a shell company, and it was still being used. He saw active payments from a bank account bearing that name to the utility company. The power was on even though the building itself appeared uninhabited.

Alex hacked into the servers used by Golden Rose, then set his bots loose to find anything they could use to connect the cases. They looked for contact addresses, names, phone numbers, and bank accounts, among other things.

"Alex," Meghan said, pulling him back to the present.

"Yeah, what's up?" he asked, trying to act innocent.

Meghan's phone rang again. "We're still not done, Wren."

"Let's go get dinner later," Alex said.

"Maybe," she said, distracted by the phone.

Yes, score.

Meghan answered the phone. "Malone." There was a pause,

then Meghan said, "What do you mean Madeline is missing?" Meghan headed back toward her office.

Alex wanted to ask Meghan about Koshy, but he was already walking a fine line and now Maxwell was in the wind. Alex's phone dinged. It was Vincent.

> VINCENT: Redman and team can be in NYC in two hours. I'm sending them to Valhalla
> ALEX: 10-4, sending you email with possible location—B can brief them when they arrive
> VINCENT: Affirmative

Alex really hoped this wasn't the biggest mistake of his life. After sending the email to Vincent, he saw a new email from one of his dark web contacts. Alex opened the email.

> TO: Ranger 8
> FROM: Black Ops Bravo
> SUBJECT: Hit ordered
> Ranger 8,
> Word on the wire is a hit just went out for FBI Special Agent Scott Bishop.
> Bravo

Fuck.

32

BISHOP

Bishop and Kat hadn't been at Vincent's house for more than five minutes when Bishop got a text from Alex.

RANGER8: The internet at Valhalla is safe but Kat is using her real device, which is pinging a cell tower. If someone were looking, they could find her. She needs to shut down the cellular on her tablet
BISHOP: Copy that...any update on the address?
RANGER8: V contracted Patrick Redman's team. They are flying in now. Expect them in two hours
BISHOP: 10-4
RANGER8: There's something up with Madeline...I heard Meghan say she was MIA
RANGER8: Oh, apparently there's a hit out on you, so don't die

What the fuck? How did Alex know there was a hit out on him? He needed answers.

BISHOP: How do you know this?

RANGER8: Dark web—don't ask
BISHOP: Who put out the hit?
RANGER8: Not sure, but I've sent out inquiries…any guesses?

Bishop had to think for a minute. He really didn't have any clue who'd want him dead and have access to a hit man. Alex said Madeline was MIA—was that connected? He replied to Alex.

BISHOP: No clue…but what's up with Madeline?
RANGER8: Only just heard, no details yet
BISHOP: Any word from Meghan about the case?
RANGER8: Check your email…and Redman will need a briefing, he only has minimal info
BISHOP: Roger that

Bishop wasn't sure how he felt about hiring mercenaries to handle the situation, but he could do nothing while he was still wanted by the FBI. Redman and his crew would need to be careful. This wasn't a third world country where they could pay off local police. They would have to be stealthy. Fuck, he hated the current situation. He should call Tyson and turn himself in. Vincent would get him a private flight to Chicago if he asked, but leaving New York wasn't the kind of thing an innocent man would do. He could bring Tyson here, but that, too, would cause complications at a hearing. It implied that Bishop thought the NYC office was corrupt, or that he was guilty and trying to get preferential treatment.

Bishop checked his email. He scanned Alex's info. Madeline was working overtime to get him convicted for this crime. Why was she so bent on this? She also claimed his service weapon had been used, which was bullshit. He had his weapon on him, and he hadn't shot Jerry.

Searching for Kat, he found her in the living room. She was sitting on the couch, using her tablet.

Kat was having a hard time settling down. Bishop could tell she was worried about her friend.

"Hey, Alex texted. We need to turn off the cellular on your tablet," Bishop said.

"Dammit. I wasn't thinking," Kat said.

She looked flustered as she tapped and swiped at the screen.

Bishop took the tablet. "Let me do it."

Kat rubbed her temples. "Thanks," she said. "Any other update?"

"Just a lot of what-the-fuck."

"That good, huh," Kat said.

"Yep."

"How exactly did everything get so fucked up?" Kat asked, in all seriousness.

"No clue, but in case we needed something else to deal with, according to Alex there's also a hit out for me," Bishop said.

"A hit? You mean like a hitman?"

Bishop nodded.

"Is it Jayda?"

Bishop shrugged. "No idea. Alex is still looking into it."

"I feel so lost in all of this," Kat said. "I don't even understand who's involved."

Bishop could help her with that. He wrapped his arm around her, leaning back against the couch.

"While we wait on Alex, I'll try to explain what's been happening. Some of this you've figured out, but in case it isn't clear how it's connected, I'll go over what we know. Okay?"

Kat settled back against him. "I'd appreciate that."

"I work for the FBI. Ryker—the real Mr. West—was coming into the country to meet with Greyson. I look enough like him that we decided to take the meeting in his place. He had a warrant out for him in Texas. We used that to arrest him at the airport."

"That's how you became Ryker West?"

"Yes. Then I met you at the restaurant and mistakenly believed you were my escort," Bishop said.

"How did you get that wrong, exactly?" Kat asked, humor in her eyes.

"Greyson was the one that provided the escort—a perk of doing business with him. I only had a description," Bishop said.

"Mr. Greyson, my boss, hired the escort?"

"Yes."

Bishop could tell Kat wasn't sold on the idea, but he moved on.

"The team lead on the op, Madeline 'Mad Max' Maxwell, somehow let Ryker escape custody, and got Jerry killed. Jerry was a rookie agent working on the team. The higher ups think I killed him—among other things. Madeline is responsible for most of this, and now she's missing."

"That's why the safe house wasn't safe?"

Bishop nodded.

"And Ryker escaped custody and showed for the meeting with Greyson. How did he know?" Kat asked.

"He didn't, but he's CIA so he decided to continue with his original plan, not realizing that I was pretending to be him."

"Ryker is CIA? Why was he in FBI custody if he's CIA?" Kat asked. "And that means Jayda was there to kill a CIA agent. Who hired her?"

"I've got a theory about that," Bishop said. "Greyson was working with Ana Ivanov. Did you ever meet her?"

"Once or twice, but she wasn't part of the firm, only a friend of Mr. Greyson's."

"Ana Ivanov is the de facto leader of the Ivanov clan. She's an oligarch that, since her father's recent death, is in charge of many illegal operations around the world. I suspect she was more than a friend to Greyson. Greyson may have been working for her, or she was using him to help other oligarchs hide their money. I just don't know why she would have wanted Ryker killed unless she knew he was CIA."

"What was Mr. Greyson into?"

"Money laundering," Bishop said.

"Greyson's money-laundering activities were why West wanted to see him. But, if West isn't really a bad guy, does that mean he is somehow a good guy?" Kat asked.

Bishop wasn't sure what to say. CIA work wasn't always clean cut. Ryker could have been tasked with destabilizing a region, or as part of his cover he might be working for a bad guy the CIA was watching. There were too many options to speculate on a plausible one in this case.

"Above my pay grade," Bishop said.

"Then it's above my pay grade, too," she said.

33

KAT

Kat wasn't sure what to do with all the new information. West was CIA. Mr. Sexy was FBI. There were other agents, too. Madeline, who Bishop called Mad Max, and made his life hell. Then there was the agent that died, which was somehow tied to Bishop and the reason the safe house was compromised. And Rip was being held by a killer—the same killer that killed Mr. Greyson, who'd already tried to kill West, and had killed Kat's blind date, some guy named Smith.

Kat's head was dizzy with all the information. And she couldn't use her tablet to search for anything. She wanted to know where Rip was located. She wanted him back healthy and safe. She didn't want anyone else to die.

"What's the plan to get Rip back?" Kat asked.

"Vincent's sending a security detail. Alex will have Rip's address by the time they get here. They'll make the plan, okay?" Bishop said.

"Okay," Kat said, moisture gathering in her eyes. "What if she's already killed him?"

"You can't think like that. We have to assume that he's still alive. We'll try to take her down either way, but until we have confirmation, we're going on the basis that he's alive and this is a rescue."

"What if he doesn't make it? What if we can't find him in time? What if we do everything she wants and she kills him anyway?"

Bishop snuggled in closer. "Shhh," he said. "She has no leverage if she kills him."

"What if she hurts him?"

Bishop kissed Kat on the top of the head and held her tighter. "The security team is good. We've gotten men out of tougher situations. Rip will be okay."

"What if he's not?" Kat asked, several tears rolling down her cheeks.

Kat wasn't sure what she would do if Rip didn't make it. She was right there with Bishop, but she'd had days of what the fuck. She needed everything to go back to normal. The vulnerable feeling she had, the unease about everything—she felt like she was reaching a breaking point. She had to hold on and not let this destroy her, but it was getting hard to stay focused and positive.

Kat circled her arms around Bishop's waist, holding him as tight as he was holding her. She liked the feeling of his strong arms wrapped around her. She didn't feel alone or scared when he was with her, which was just stupid. He was the definition of dangerous. He probably skydived to the office every day, drove fast cars, and knew a hundred different ways to kill a man with his bare hands. And someone wanted him dead—contract killer dead. He wasn't the safe, white picket fence Kat had been looking for. He was every thrill seeking bad first date she'd ever had, rolled into one. He wasn't in her plans, so how could he be the right guy for her?

Kat moved to get up.

"Where are you going?" Bishop asked, holding on an extra moment before letting her go.

"I need time to think. You aren't the guy I'm looking for. I need normal, stable, boring. I don't need bullets and assassins and dirty FBI agents."

Kat backed up. Bishop stood. Reaching out, he took her hand before she could get too far away.

"I'm not some adrenaline junky waiting for my next fix," Bishop said. "This situation is not my normal."

"So being an FBI agent—going after bad guys—that's not your normal?" Kat asked.

Bishop hesitated.

"I need a safe, uncomplicated life."

Bishop pulled Kat in for a hug. "I want all of those things for you," he said. "Believe it or not, this is actually my low-risk job."

Kat snorted.

"That's not really helping is it?"

Kat shook her head. "What the hell was your high-risk job?"

Bishop led Kat back to the couch. He wiped the tears from her cheeks. "I graduated high school at sixteen, and no, it wasn't because I was some child genius. I was homeschooled, but Mom didn't buy into the whole summer vacation concept."

"You were home schooled year-round?" Kat asked. "I thought you said that pick-up line was from middle school?"

Bishop smiled. "We had socializing activities like school dances."

"With other home schoolers?"

Bishop nodded. "And there was no slacking. You got up, got busy, and got your work done. No excuses, no exceptions. Seven days a week. Boot camp was a cake walk compared to my mom's routine."

"You had no play time?"

"It wasn't as bad as it sounds, just relentless, and structured. We had exactly one hour every day to run around outside. Forty-five minutes to play games. Two hours to read or craft or paint. Six hours for school subjects, which we could pick from a list, but had to include the basics. For a while, my elective was public speaking—my sisters wanted to kill me."

"How much time did you spend learning to dance? I seem to remember you killing it on the dance floor."

Bishop laughed. "With four older sisters. I was press ganged into it starting at age twelve. I blame it on the growth spurt."

Kat laughed. "So the dancing thing wasn't just part of your cover."

He shook his head. "Nope, that was one-hundred percent Scott Bishop."

Kat felt comfortable around him. She knew it was a bad plan, but she relaxed into him. "Okay, so home school wasn't the high-risk job, right?"

"No, but it did give me a serious work ethic. The high-risk job came after college. I'd always considered joining the military, but I couldn't enlist at sixteen, so I went to university and almost lost my freedom."

Kat looked up into his eyes. "How?"

"Without my drill sergeant, AKA Mom," he said with a smile, "I made a few bad choices. I got arrested for pulling a stupid prank on another team's mascot. I was almost expelled. My mother made me quit the fraternity and focus on school. She also reminded the school that I was still a minor."

"You joined a fraternity at sixteen?"

"Technically, I was seventeen and a half, but they assumed I was older—growth spurt, remember. I was already six-three at thirteen."

"Okay, so your mom saved your ass. Then what?"

"I got back to what I knew. I finished my mechanical engineering degree at nineteen and signed up for the military. It changed my life. And almost got me killed."

"What happened?" Kat asked.

"There's a lot I can't talk about, but I was an Army Ranger doing black ops assignments outside the country. We had a mission go as far wrong as one can go. That's when Alex lost part of his leg. We all almost died. Then the allegations started. We were accused of treason and thrown in the brig. Footage surfaced of the incident, but it was doctored to include scenes from a different op—that we weren't a part of. Charges were eventually dropped, but there has always been some doubt of our innocence."

"That's horrible. Is that why you aren't in the military?"

"We were forced out, which is why I now work for my low-risk job at the FBI."

"Low risk, right," Kat said, snuggling in closer. "I think I should call you Mr. Dangerous instead of Mr. Sexy."

34

BISHOP

Bishop wasn't sure what he thought about his new moniker. He liked it when Kat called him Mr. Sexy. Mr. Dangerous wasn't him. Mr. Ready-And-Prepared-For-Damn-Near-Anything was closer to the truth. He'd never be Mr. Boring, there was no doubt about that. It wasn't like Kat was skittish or anxiety ridden, and the last few days had been more complicated than any normal person should reasonably have to handle. But she was hanging in there. She was a trooper, but that didn't mean she would be able to deal with a long-term relationship with a guy that carried a gun for a living.

It wasn't fair to expect her to want that kind of life. He had to get her through this, save her roommate, and let her go.

The idea of never seeing her again hurt more than Bishop wanted to admit. He loved the way she felt, snuggled safely in his arms. If he could keep her cocooned in a protected bubble he would, but that wasn't reality, and no woman would want that.

He didn't even know how to handle the idea of protecting her forever—making her his. He'd spent so much time working on his career. First in the Army, then for the FBI. He'd had friends with benefits—like Madeline—but nothing that lasted long. Partly because he never wanted it to last long.

Then he'd met Kat. She was like a breath of fresh air. He'd wanted to save her from a life of bad choices that led her to being an escort. Then when he discovered she wasn't an escort, he wasn't sure what to do. She didn't technically need saving, but he still wanted to save her. He wanted her to be his.

Bishop couldn't do that to her.

Kat wanted a normal life. Bishop wasn't sure he'd ever be normal.

"When will the security team be here?" Kat asked.

"Soon."

"I'm glad you're not really the kind of guy that thought I was a hooker," Kat said.

Bishop chuckled. "I'm glad you're not a hooker."

Kat giggled.

"I just want Rip safe. I want to be safe. I want you safe. And I want you out of trouble with the FBI. Jayda is the one that killed Greyson and Smith. She should be their focus, not you. When all of this shit is settled, when my life is back to normal and your name has been cleared, I want to go dancing with you again."

Bishops arms tightened around her. "I'd like that," he said. "I'd like that a lot." He kissed her on the top of the head.

Bishop wasn't sure how long they stayed like that on the sofa, just holding each other, but too soon there was a knock on the door.

Bishop shifted to get up. "Stay here and stay quiet," he said.

Taking his gun from the coffee table, he held it at the ready as he walked toward the door. Checking the peephole, he lowered the gun.

"Who is it?" Kat asked.

"It's Redman and his team."

Bishop opened the door. Four men wearing matte black head-to-toe tactical gear came in. They all had helmets on and several looked to be fitted with night vision goggles. They were all carrying assault weapons.

Bishop shook Redman's hand. "Patrick, good to see you again."

Patrick handed Bishop a bag. "Alex sent this. He also gave us the address to the warehouse in New Jersey where he believes the roommate is being held."

Kat stood up. "You know where Rip is?"

"We believe we do, ma'am," Redman said.

"Fantastic," Bishop said.

"Awesome," Kat said.

"We'll use the office," Bishop said. "Kat, you can join us if you want, but you may prefer not knowing."

"I have a separate tactical team ready to hit the building," Patrick said. "As soon as it's dark enough and you approve the plan, we'll bring up comms and link to video of the raid."

"I want to see that," Kat said.

Bishop held out his hand for Kat to take. "Let's go save your friend."

JAYDA

"Where the fuck are your friends, pretty boy?" Jayda yelled at Rip, who was tied to the radiator in the warehouse office. "Can't your girl follow simple directions? She should have come here right away. Unless she doesn't care for you."

"Fuck you," Rip said.

Jayda laughed. "Oh, have I hurt the pretty baby's feelings. Boo hoo."

"Kat won't come here. I left her a hidden message. She'll know it isn't safe."

Jayda considered this for a moment but discounted it. She'd seen what was written on the board. It was very clear, but maybe he meant something else? "What did you do?" Jayda asked.

Rip laughed. "Nothing you'll ever figure out."

Jayda walked over to Rip and smacked him hard across the face with her weapon.

"Fuck," he cursed.

"Should I beat it out of you? Should I remove your pretty boy features? Kill your modeling career?"

"Fuck you. We both know you plan to kill me, so why would I help you?" Rip asked.

Jayda crouched down to eye level with Rip. She stroked his cheek, taking care to avoid his bruises. "Oh, my sweet. You don't want me to get angry with you. I could make you beg for death. Would you like for me to do that?" Jayda moved her hand to Rip's groin. Lowering her voice, she rubbed her hand between his legs, down his shaft. "There are things I could do that would make you crave pain—beg for it—all while cumming so hard you'd pray for the agony to never stop. I could do that to you. I could make you crave the bite of a whip. I could train you to only respond to the heat of the lash on your genitals. Would you like that, my sweet? Would you like for me to own your soul?"

Jayda continued to rub Rip through his pants. She smiled as he tried to stay in control. His soft grunts told her everything she needed to know. Leaning in, she put pressure on his hardening erection. He shifted to try and get away, but he was too securely tied.

"You are helpless to stop me," she said.

"Fuck you, psycho," he cried out.

Jayda increased the tempo. She'd spent two years perfecting her talents. She never missed a beat, never failed to force satisfaction. She'd learned early on that she could only take control if they were getting what they didn't know they wanted. If she could get the John off with her hand, he'd go, and leave her alone. The pretty boy roommate didn't stand a chance.

Jayda could tell that he was getting close. Breathing into his ear, she said, "You like that don't you? You need it—want it. Beg me for it."

"No," he rasped.

Jayda chuckled, refocusing her efforts. "Beg me. Tell me how much you want it. Tell me. Say, faster, Jayda. Say, make me cum, Jayda. Beg me, pretty boy, or I'll keep you on the edge for hours."

Rip whimpered. "Please."

"Please what? Please stop?" Jayda pretended to move her hand away.

"No," Rip said. "Please, Jayda. Please finish."

Leaning in to put her mouth right beside his ear, she said, "Oh, my sweet, you are very naughty. If I were keeping you. I would punish you for your lack of originality." Jayda added the right pressure, ramping up the heat—letting him almost peak. "I could have so much fun with you. I could keep you as my slave. Would you like that?" When Rip didn't respond, Jayda eased the pressure and removed the friction. Without that, he'd never release.

"No, please," Rip begged. "Please, Jayda."

Caressing his face again, she smiled, locking her eyes with his. "No, my sweet. You must not be rewarded, but maybe I will change my mind later."

Jayda gave Rip two light slaps on the face, leaving him with a painful looking erection. She laughed as she left him alone in the room.

Jayda checked that the explosives were ready, and that the wireless network was up. If she had to leave the building, she'd engage the booby trap. If Kat arrived while she was gone, the entire building would go boom and that would be that. She considered using that plan and leaving now but being able to look your mark in the eye was so much more satisfying. Also, she'd lose her warehouse if she did that, and this property had been useful on more than one occasion.

Jayda's phone chimed with an incoming text. She opened the texting app and saw that it was a message from Madeline.

FBI_FOOL: Adjustment needed. Additional target:
Meghan Malone, FBI, Chicago…can you handle both?

Fucking hell. Did Madeline think Ana had nothing better to do than kill off FBI agents? Jayda texted back.

JAYDA: I'll need to freelance the second job, but it can be
        done. Price is double
FBI_FOOL: 25% now, the remainder of the deposit
        tomorrow?

Was Madeline losing it? She'd never had an issue getting money before. Jayda wasn't sure she should trust her, but what was one more hit? Jayda had to keep Madeline happy or Jayda's picture could wind up splashed all over the news channels, making it impossible to get out of the city.
Jayda texted back.

JAYDA: Only this once
FBI_FOOL: Sending money now

Jayda clicked over to her bank account and saw the $2500 payment from Madeline. Returning to the chat, she finished the transaction.

JAYDA: Send her whereabouts and a photograph. Any
        update on Bishop? Your details have been light
FBI_FOOL: Nothing new
JAYDA: What are you doing to track him? What about
        Kaitlyn, do you have any leads on her?
FBI_FOOL: No investigation on the secretary. They are
        treating her as a hostage

These people were idiots. Or maybe it was just Madeline. Jayda tried not to be too condescending in her reply.

JAYDA: Unless you believe she is a prisoner, you need to be
        looking for her too
FBI_FOOL: Not my op anymore. I'm doing my best to

keep the police from showing your photo. Finding Bishop is on you

Fuck. It was a good thing Jayda had her own plan, otherwise she'd be screwed. Madeline was a flake and may need to be handled sooner rather than later, but for the moment she'd paid a deposit, which meant Jayda would contact Evgeni about doing the hit.

Jayda forwarded Madeline's email with Meghan Malone's info to Evgeni, then switched over to Evgeni's chat session.

JAYDA: Are you available to assist?
EVGENI: I received your request. My price, minus the family discount. Should I proceed?
JAYDA: Yes, my sweet. Handle Malone and let me know when you're done. Partial payment has already been received. You will be paid upon immediate completion of job
EVGENI: Consider it done. Proof will be emailed

At least that was one thing Jayda no longer had to worry about. Evgeni was a true professional and he never missed his mark. Meghan Malone was as good as dead.

Jayda contacted one of her hackers to try and find Bishop. If the FBI weren't going to help, she needed her own spies working the op—no matter the cost. She should have contacted them earlier, but she was sure the text to Kat would have sent her scurrying to the apartment to save Rip. Of course, Bishop could be keeping her away. Would nothing work out as she'd planned?

36

BISHOP

Patrick Redman had all six monitors of Vincent's massive display wall lit up. One was a poor-quality view of the warehouse, another had building schematics, and another had a picture of Jayda taken from the security cameras in Greyson's building and Rip from his driver's license.

Vincent's office/study was more like a command center. Similar to a system Alex had set up for Drake's various properties, it was wired to monitor the house's security as well as a few other buildings Vincent owned around the city. The monitors made it easy to allow multiple scenes to be displayed at once. The tactical team going in for the rescue would be wearing body cameras, which meant everyone could see the entire operation as it went down, from the safety of the sanctuary.

The lone video camera near the warehouse was from a nearby business. Alex had helped Redman's tech guy hack into it. The picture was a little grainy and not really aimed to watch the warehouse, but it allowed the team to confirm someone was in the building.

Redman and his guys were top-notch and could totally handle the situation, but the ex-Army Ranger in Bishop wished he was going in with the team. Bishop would be able to follow the progress, which meant he wasn't going to be left in the dark, but the call was still there to be in the thick of things. It had been several years since he had done this type of rescue work with a team of trained soldiers. He'd always miss it, but this wasn't his op. The FBI had an APB out for him, an unknown player wanted him dead, and his only champions weren't in a position to assist with the cluster of issues he now faced. He was stuck at the sanctuary until his name could be cleared. Getting Jayda would be a step in the right direction, but Bishop wasn't sure she'd be enough to clear his name. The issue of Jerry's death was more pressing, and there was no indication it could be tied to Jayda—that would be too easy. Greyson's death was only partially connected to Bishop's real trouble.

"What kind of ammo are they using?" Bishop asked.

"Standard non-lethal darts," Patrick said. "This is strictly capture and rescue."

"Good," Bishop said. He squeezed Kat's hand. She looked relieved as well.

"As you can see from the schematics," Patrick said, pointing at one of the monitors, "there are two entrances. Both lead into the warehouse's administrative part, which consists of two offices, a restroom, and a small storage closet. The warehouse itself has two main cargo bays with a giant rolling door at the back and front. We'll use the smaller side doors for entry during the op."

"How are you getting to the site?" Bishop asked.

"We'll be dropping in from helos," Patrick said.

"Won't that be too loud?"

Patrick shook his head. "We'll stay high and rappel down. The amount of time we're within range to be heard will be minimal and should sound like a fly over. If the compound was bigger, or had more men on the ground, we'd take a different approach. As it stands, everything should be fine."

"When Alex sent the camera feed info, he said the building had a wireless network set up," Bishop said. "What's that for?"

Patrick shrugged. "It could be a simple Wi-Fi set up for her phone. We're not sure."

One of the commandos standing off to the side said, "It could also be a relay to allow remote detonation."

Patrick nodded. "Considering Jayda is onsite, which we will confirm prior to entry, I believe any remote detonation scenario is unlikely. We'll be deploying a standard jamming technology either way, which should prevent any remote destruction of the building. No one plans to die here."

"Copy that," Bishop said.

Patrick and his team had everything under control. Bishop assumed Alex was also wired into the op, but he wanted to touch base. Bringing up his texting app he messaged Alex.

>   BISHOP: Are you jacked in to the call?
>   RANGER8: Audio only for now, but I'm about to drop off
>   —there's something big happening in the office
>   BISHOP: Related to me?
>   RANGER8: I'll let you know
>   BISHOP: One more thing. How many buildings near the
>   warehouse are occupied?
>   RANGER8: Most are deserted. Why?
>   BISHOP: Wireless network. Speculation there could be
>   explosives
>   RANGER8: I can cut the power to that building if needed,
>   but the jammers should cover it
>   BISHOP: 10-4

"Alex says most of the buildings around the warehouse are deserted," Bishop said, "but I want your team to confirm before they enter the warehouse. If there is any possibility at all this can't be a simple snatch and grab, I'll have to notify the FBI or local police."

Kat hugged Bishop's arm. He knew she was worried about Rip, but Bishop couldn't risk Redman's team and any local bystanders if the situation didn't look safe. He squeezed her hand for comfort.

"Understood," Patrick said. "We'll thermal image the area before we drop."

"I trust your team, but if anything has the potential to go sideways, I want you to retreat."

"Once we're on the ground, we'll assess the situation," Patrick said. "If anything looks hinky, we'll abort."

Bishop was possibly making a career-ending move, but Jayda was expecting Kat to rescue her friend. The minute she decided that wasn't going to happen she'd cut and run. Rip wouldn't survive in that case. Bishop knew the FBI wouldn't be able to pull a tactical team together fast enough to get Rip out. This was the only option to save Rip.

Bishop's phone dinged with an incoming text. It was from Alex.

> RANGER8: Meghan provided her final report to Reece.
> Madeline's days are numbered
> BISHOP: In what way?
> RANGER8: Meghan found the original paperwork Jerry submitted. Madeline was requesting intel on ops she had no valid reason to see. They think she might be linked to Ana Ivanov

What the hell? Bishop knew Madeline was ambitious, but a double agent? He texted for clarification.

> BISHOP: What did she request?
> RANGER8: She requested status updates on Tyson's

investigation, specifically status on Evgeni Petrov. She requested money to cover renting an office near the FBI building in Chicago, but that office wasn't listed on official paperwork
BISHOP: Who was using the office?
RANGER8: Paperwork from the building manager says Ana Ivanov, but surveillance shows that no one has entered the property since it was rented. Meghan has requested a warrant to search the premises. They plan to raid the place tomorrow
BISHOP: Why would Ana want an update about Evgeni or an office near the FBI in Chicago?
RANGER8: It may not have been Ana. Madeline's work phone texts are being pulled and analyzed. It may be days before they have the complete picture
RANGER8: She recently ordered cocaine from her new underworld friend
BISHOP: Interesting. Anything new about Jerry?
RANGER8: Meghan has requested ballistics on all the guns at the safe house, including Madeline's. The system says the slug pulled out of Jerry matches your gun, but she's requested new ballistics tests for all weapons

Bishop instinctively felt for his gun—his FBI-issued Glock. The gun that needed to get back to FBI headquarters to clear him of the murder charge. He snapped a quick picture of the serial number, then texted that to Alex.

BISHOP: I've sent a picture of my serial number—maybe that will help
BISHOP: Will Reece approve the ballistics tests?
RANGER8: At this point he has no choice. Madeline is MIA and the paper trail paints her as a possible traitor. Meghan says he'll cooperate

BISHOP: I'll turn myself in tomorrow morning. If they inspect my gun, they'll know it isn't the weapon that killed Jerry. Hopefully that will be enough to clear my name—now that Madeline is under suspicion

RANGER8: 10-4…now I just have to convince Meghan to have dinner with me :)

BISHOP: Office fraternization is discouraged, loverboy

RANGER8: You're currently holed up with your witness, ace…care to throw more stones ;)

BISHOP: LOL—see you soon

Bishop wasn't out of the woods yet, but now there was light at the end of the tunnel. He still might not make it out of this unscathed, but he wouldn't go down for Jerry's murder.

Bishop was surprised to learn about the drugs. Ryker had indicated Madeline had been high when she talked to him. Bishop had always known her to be high strung, but he'd never suspected drugs before. Drugs or not, her story was being discredited. He didn't want to believe that Madeline had killed a fellow agent, but Bishop knew he hadn't done it, and if a search in the FBI database hit a gun registered to any agent, that meant it wasn't Ryker. Madeline was the only answer that made sense.

Bishop considered reaching out to Ryker but decided against it. There was too much risk in trying to contact him. For now, he'd let Patrick and his guys complete the mission. If the op ran smoothly, Kat would have her roommate back tonight, and Bishop would be in FBI custody tomorrow morning.

37

EVGENI

Evgeni was perched atop a building across from a small bistro near the FBI headquarters in Chicago. He was on the hunt for Meghan Malone, a job he was doing at Jayda's request. He'd planned to lay in wait with his sniper rifle and take the shot as she left the building for the night, but apparently she was working late.

When she finally left the office, she wasn't alone. She and a young guy were now sitting in outside seating at a small cafe near the FBI building.

Evgeni set up his remote listening antenna and pointed it at the couple. With clear line of sight their conversation could easily be heard using the amplified receiver. He switched on the listening device and began to line up his shot. If he could get a clear shot, he'd take her out and avoid any collateral damage. Evgeni wasn't concerned about hitting bystanders, but in today's world of mass shootings a simple hit could go south quickly. Evgeni was willing to risk it. Even this close to the FBI headquarters, a single gunshot in a controlled environment shouldn't get the terrorist treatment.

Evgeni heard the waiter leave. He turned his attention to their conversation.

"This is breaking all of my rules, Wren," Meghan Malone said.

For a second, Evgeni thought he was hearing a ghost. A voice from a decade ago—a voice that was already dead. Evgeni studied the scene through his scope.

The guy sitting beside her smiled. He was a handsome young man, the kind of guy who had no trouble attracting women. The kind of guy Evgeni hated on principle. Maybe he'd do a twofer, one fee, two dead. Evgeni didn't usually take out someone for no money, but it might throw the authorities off of his scent if both were hit.

"Meghan, this is just like lunch only later," Wren said.

Meghan laughed. "Don't get used to it. I don't make a habit of fraternizing with the people I work with, Alex."

That voice—it was so familiar. It reminded him of Jocelyn, but the face wasn't the same. He'd never seen this woman before Jayda sent him the photo. He had to stop seeing ghosts. This wasn't Jocelyn Novak—she'd been killed six years ago by one of Evgeni's competitors.

"But I'm just a consultant," Alex Wren said, pulling Evgeni away from his thoughts of the past. "I'll be out of the office before you know it."

"So does that mean this is going to be a regular occurrence?" she asked.

Evgeni was watching her reactions.

The guy shrugged. "Do you want it to be?"

It can't be her, can it?

"Bishop's name will be cleared soon," Alex said. "So you won't have to arrest my best friend—which would be awkward."

She laughed. "He hasn't been cleared yet, but I agree. Madeline is MIA. Her service weapon should have been checked."

"They'll find her, right?"

"If she's gone off the reservation, who knows. She was always high strung, but this is loco even for her."

The guy with Malone was one of Bishop's friends. Bishop was one of the FBI agents that tried to help Holden—who'd become romantically involved with Drake, another friend of theirs that owned a nightclub in Chicago. Evgeni hated that Holden had to die, but it couldn't be helped. She'd seen his face.

Evgeni tuned out of their conversation. It was like the start to a sappy romantic comedy where the standoffish girl eventually gets persuaded to date by the charismatic cute guy. Total bullshit in Evgeni's experience. He had a job to do and, ghost or not, Meghan Malone would die tonight.

Evgeni took a few calming breaths and lined up his shot. He had one try to make this a simple solution. His plan was to hit Meghan in the chest. It was less dramatic than a headshot, but from Evgeni's vantage point, a shot to the chest should embed in the side of the building, not crash through the window behind her.

He was close enough to the target that natural forces like wind weren't going to affect his shot. Although Chicago was called the Windy City for a reason, today the weather was mild. It took skill to sniper someone at any distance, but this was one of the easier shots he'd ever have to make.

Evgeni slowed his breathing to prepare for the shot. He breathed in, then out, then one long breath in. Hold. Pull the trigger.

As he watched, his scope whited out. Looking up, he saw a white panel van pull to a stop in front of the bistro. The bullet ricocheted off the van, hitting a street light, which sent a few sparks flying and caused the light to go out. As the van drove off, Evgeni listened for their reaction.

"What was that?" Meghan said.

"Fuck," Evgeni mumbled, lining up a new shot.

Most of the sidewalk was now in shadow, but Evgeni could

still see Meghan and her date. They were both being covered by the outside lighting at the bistro. With less prep, he confirmed his second shot and pulled the trigger, just as Meghan moved. The bullet missed her heart, but she was hit.

Evgeni heard screams from the chaos below. Fuck, he had to turn this into something else, which meant he'd need to leave town ASAP. He hit the button to summon his Uber, then settled in to make this an event no one would understand or forget.

With confusion in full swing, Evgeni lined up several extra shots. None were intended to hit anyone, except the third shot which he aimed at Alex Wren's leg. He also took out the cafe's window and landed several shots at the feet of some patrons who'd not yet decided to flee. That sent them running.

Eight shots, and his days in the US were numbered. Beginning with his riffle, Evgeni hurriedly started packing his equipment to leave. As he closed and snapped his gun case shut, he heard a name.

"Simon Novak," Alex yelled, over the chaos. "Who's Simon Novak?"

"Fuck," Evgeni muttered.

He'd been right. It was Jocelyn. How was that possible? She was supposed to be dead. Did Novak know she lived?

Evgeni couldn't listen longer, he had to get moving. He packed away his listening device as his phone beeped to indicate his Uber had arrived.

Evgeni hurriedly took the stairs down the building, exiting on the opposite side of the street from the cafe. If Meghan didn't bleed out, he'd take his info to Novak. He was sure the man would like to know that his trusted assassin, and Evgeni's arch nemesis, Townsend, had lied to him. Jocelyn Novak wasn't dead. If Meghan Malone lived, he could prove it.

The Uber Evgeni had summoned was waiting on him. Luckily, the chaos happening one street over hadn't spilled onto this road yet. He slid into the back seat, resting his trombone case on the seat beside him.

"The wait time costs extra, dude," the drive said.

"That's not a problem," Evgeni said. "Please drive."

"Whatever, man," the driver said.

Evgeni often wondered about the youth of today. Maybe he should set this particular individual straight. Maybe explain to him how manners make the man. But unfortunately, he didn't have time for that this trip. He took a screenshot of the Uber app with the driver's name and car model. Maybe if he got bored and was ever in Chicago again, he would hunt the young man down for fun.

Evgeni had had very little fun lately. And now with the sniper attack, he needed to get out of the country. He'd message Jayda to let her know about Meghan. The shot had been messy. He should have taken another kill shot but at least now the incident would look like a random act of violence, not an attempt to kill an FBI agent. He wondered who made Meghan's IDs. The FBI had an imposter working for them. Evgeni wondered if they knew.

He opened his chat and selected Jayda's name.

EVGENI: Malone is hit, status unknown. Must depart posthaste. Will be unable to confirm
JAYDA: This isn't like you, my sweet. Are you unable to complete the mission?
EVGENI: If she dies I expect payment, otherwise c'est la vie

Evgeni had no intention of telling Jayda the truth about Meghan's real identity. He'd solve the mystery of Jocelyn Novak on his own.

Jayda texted back.

JAYDA: What about my IDs

EVGENI: Fee has been paid, contact JJ
JAYDA: Ana is your problem
EVGENI: Understood

Jayda was on her own. Evgeni had to save himself first. For now, Ana was a low priority. He needed to leave the country. He'd find out where Simon Novak called home and make his way there.

38

REECE

ADIC Reece Patterson wasn't convinced his career would survive this storm. He'd majorly fucked up by promoting Madeline Maxwell. In his entire career at the FBI he'd never once let his dick make a decision about personnel, but damn, Madeline had been different. She'd played him, but even after she dropped him to focus on her new opportunities, he hadn't realized just how bad his choice had been. The first indication should have been when Meghan Malone requested a transfer. Now he was sitting on an epic fail scenario that could end his career.

He'd typed up a resignation letter this morning. That was before he received Meghan's report on Madeline's op. There would be no resignation to save him. He'd have to ride this tsunami to its bitter end.

Reece picked up his office phone and dialed Roger Watts, the agent he'd assigned to fix this cluster.

"Yes, sir. Perfect timing," Watts said.

"Do we have a location on Bishop or the girl?" Reece asked.

"Yes, the warrant went through on her cell records. We have a ping from two hours ago near a house owned by Vincent York—a known associate of Bishop."

"You think Bishop is there?"

"We have a team ready to find out. You just need to give the word."

Reece had to bring the agent in. Even if Meghan's report was correct and Madeline was responsible for Jerry's death, there was an APB out for Bishop. This loose end had to be tied up.

"What did we find out about the roommate?" Reece asked.

"He's not at the apartment. A neighbor said he left with a dark-haired female before Kaitlyn returned with Bishop to the apartment. The woman ID'd Bishop from a photo. But that was hours ago," Watts said.

"Who was the dark-haired female?"

"Unknown, but at the moment we don't think it's related."

"Did you show the neighbor pictures of Ivanov or the Dragon?" Reece asked.

"She reminded me that she said the woman had dark hair."

Your basic unreliable witness. "Okay, for now let's assume he's inconsequential to the case. Move forward with the op to pick up Bishop. I'll inform the communications department in case the York family complain about the raid."

"That should only be a problem if Bishop isn't there," Watts said. "We'll check with thermal imaging before we storm the place."

"Sounds good. Keep me informed."

"Will do."

Reece ended the call, then started sending emails. He'd implement all of Meghan Malone's suggestions and put out an APB for Madeline Maxwell. If she had killed her own agent, he'd take her down—no matter the cost to his own career. He owed it to Osborn for putting him in that situation.

Reece's phone rang. It was an unknown number. He'd been dreading this call all day. He was about to get his ass chewed out for not recognizing they had a fucking CIA operative on their hands. At least this mistake wasn't squarely on his shoulders. Madeline had done a good job of keeping the new parameters of her mission on the down low. It didn't absolve him of the blowback, but it wouldn't get him fired.

Taking a deep breath, he answered the phone.

39

KAT

Kat's stomach was in knots worrying about Rip. The security detail seemed very competent, but Kat wasn't exactly sure how she should feel about all of this. At least they were using non-lethal darts so they couldn't accidentally kill Rip. Bishop made her feel safe but the whole situation with all the guns and killing and everything else was just a major disaster. How was her life supposed to go back to normal if Rip didn't make it? God, she didn't even have a job anymore, and if Rip didn't come back she'd be homeless. She couldn't afford the apartment on her own.

Stop. Calm down. Breathe.

Kat looked over at Bishop who was studying the monitors on the wall. Vincent's office, and Kat uses that term very lightly, was a mini version of NORAD. It was like this room was *designed* to watch a team of black ops mercenaries helicopter in to do a rescue.

Kat walked over to Bishop and put her hand on his shoulder.

"Is Rip going to be okay?" she asked.

"Redman and his team are the best. If Rip can be extracted—"

"Extracted?" Kat said. What the fuck did that mean?

Bishop smiled, taking her hand in his. "If Rip can be rescued, he will be. The team is good, and they know what they're doing."

A squawking sound came from the military grade walkie-talkie on the desk.

"Everything looks good from the sky. Starting the jammer now. We should be on the ground in two."

Kat thought the guy sounded confident, but what the hell did she know. God, she hoped Rip was okay. Bishop was sure Redman's team had everything under control, but she couldn't breathe easy yet. Now came the hard part, waiting to hear that Rip was safe.

The stress of this day—no, week—was starting to wear thin. Kat just wanted to go home. She wanted Rip back, and if she was being honest, she wanted Bishop beside her in her bed. Wild and crazy Mr. Dangerous—that was who she wanted.

What an absolutely horrible time to start falling in love. Was that what she was doing? Rip had kidded her for weeks about doing the blind dating service, but she had wanted to meet a nice guy with a boring career and a white picket fence in their future. But, no, she had to meet the absolute opposite of boring career guy. She had to meet Special Agent Scott Bishop.

Kat watched the monitors. On the one showing the feed from the lone business's surveillance camera, she saw what looked like a motorcycle zoom past, but it was dark and the motorcycle didn't have any headlights so she wasn't sure. She turned to say something to Bishop, but she was interrupted by the radio.

"We're on the ground. Tear gas has been launched," the voice said.

Just as Kat heard the words from the radio, a window in the living room of the house she was in smashed. The tumbling sound of a metal can pinged along the floor in the next room. Just like in the movies, it spewed out noxious fumes as it somersaulted end over end.

Then, everything went dark.

Hands grabbed her, pulling her down. Kat screamed.

"Shhh...it's me," Bishop said.

"What the hell is happening?" she asked.

Kat started coughing from the tear gas. Her eyes were watering. She heard the slosh of water. Bishop pressed a cold wet rag to her face.

"Cover your nose and mouth. Try to keep your eyes shut. This is the FBI. We're going to get down on the ground and not move, okay."

"Okay," Kat mumbled through the cloth.

Within seconds, the sound of a battering ram and splintered wood was heard. Voices and noises were coming from every direction. Beams of light from flashlights were bouncing around the room. Several people yelled *clear*. Behind her Kat heard the radio squawk again.

"Package is secured. I repeat, package is secured. Hostile missing. Warehouse..." the sound trailed off as someone shut off the radio.

"In here," a man in the room said. "They're in here."

Another voice came in. Strong hands picked Kat up, lifting her off the ground. She dropped her wet cloth as they wrenched her arms behind her back. She heard the metal clink as the handcuffs were locked.

"Bishop," she screamed, as they marched her out of the house.

Kat was put in the back of a black sedan. The tears in her eyes were making it difficult for her to see much of anything. The lights from the street were bouncing in starburst patterns on every shiny surface, making it nearly impossible to identify anyone.

Someone got in the driver's seat and started the car.

"Where's Bishop?" she asked, but the driver didn't answer. At least Rip was okay. Redman and his team had gotten the package.

40

JAYDA

Jayda was getting frustrated. Evgeni had failed in his mission to take out Malone. The man who never failed had simply given up. Oh, Meghan might still die, but he'd left it up to fate. That was unacceptable. A professional didn't quit once they'd taken the job. Of course, if the client was dead, there would be no hit to complete. Jayda's hacker hadn't turned up any leads on Bishop or Kat, but he had turned up pictures of Greyson's shooter. Madeline had failed to protect Jayda's identity. She'd broken their pact.

Jayda needed to put this entire clusterfuck in her rearview. At least Evgeni had secured her new IDs. She was done with this city. The only loose end was Madeline. Kat was a personal target, an attempt to get Smith and Greyson's murders pinned on someone else. It had been a long shot, but Jayda's life would be a hell of a lot easier if she wasn't running from the FBI. It had caused Evgeni nothing but trouble. Jayda had hoped to avoid it, but no luck—which was starting to be her MO.

Bishop and Meghan were Madeline's targets. Bishop's job was predicated on a favor, keeping Jayda's image off the news, which Madeline failed to do. But Meghan's hit had been partially paid for. To save face Meghan had to die or the client had to fail to complete their part of the bargain. The only way to do that was to end Madeline. If she were dead, she couldn't pay Jayda's fee and the hit would be cancelled.

Jayda took a last look around the warehouse. She would arm the explosives and walk away. When someone finally came for Rip, they'd set off the explosives and die. If that was or wasn't Kat, it no longer mattered. The Jade Dragon would die tonight—after taking out the FBI fool.

With those decisions made, Jayda prepared her motorcycle to leave. As she was packing the bike, she heard the whomp-whomp-whomp sound of an incoming helicopter. She waited a second for it to pass, but it didn't. There was pause.

"Son of a bitch," Jayda muttered, pushing her bike out the side door.

Jayda armed the system. She heard what sounded like a dying video game.

She laughed. The bastards had brought a jammer. Oh well, no fireworks tonight, New Jersey.

It didn't matter. Maybe they'd still trip the system and blow themselves up—she didn't care. She needed to start reinventing herself. New hair, new name, new skills. She could relocate to Canada. Those people seemed nice. They had legalized marijuana. Maybe Jayda should start a completely new line of business. Assassin for hire was so passé.

Jayda started her bike but didn't turn on the headlight. She headed off down the road. She needed to put distance between herself and the warehouse.

Now to kill Madeline.

41

REECE

Reece was sitting in an outer office waiting for the deputy director to see him. He'd been summoned to the office shortly after the deputy director arrived. Reece saw this power play for what it was. He was being made to wait—in his own damn headquarters—because the deputy directory wasn't happy. At least the shit show hadn't made it to the director level, yet.

Reece's phone pinged. It was an email from the tech reviewing Madeline's records. He skimmed the email. The techs were able to retrieve data from Madeline's qualifying round at the Academy. The gun she used then, which according to internal records was still her service weapon, matched the ballistics currently assigned to Bishop's gun. The gun that killed Agent Osborn.

Reece shook his head. Fuck. It was too late to stop the op now.

The techs also retrieved audit logs, which indicate Bishop's gun assignment had recently changed. They didn't find the same detail on Madeline's record, which meant someone had been very sloppy in their attempt to pin a murder on a good agent. And Reece was the last to know. Preliminary results had already been emailed up the chain. They'd needed permission to search archived records. At least Reece now knew why he was waiting to talk to the deputy director.

Reece's cellphone rang. It was Watts.

"We've got Bishop and the girl, but there's a problem," Watts said.

There's a problem was not what Reece wanted to hear. "What?"

"Someone paid Patrick Redman's team to rescue Rip Taylor—Kaitlyn Fox's roommate. He was being held by Jayda Dragon in a warehouse in New Jersey."

Reece pinched the bridge of his nose. What the ever-loving fuck was he going to do with this? The techs had cleared Bishop's gun. Records had been tampered with. Madeline's assigned weapon was the one that killed Agent Osborn. Madeline, the agent he had promoted, was a murderer and he'd sent agents after Bishop. Now they had discovered that Kaitlyn's roommate had in fact been kidnapped, and fucking mercenaries had been paid to rescue him—on US soil.

"Who paid Redman?" Reece asked.

"They've lawyered up. Kaitlyn was taken to the hospital. Bishop is being brought in. How should we handle it?" Watts asked.

"No one is to touch him. I just received confirmation that he isn't the shooter. His gun didn't kill Osborn. Bring him in and keep him isolated."

"Ten-four. What about Redman?" Watts said.

"Do we have the roommate?"

"Yes, and his parents have been located and confirmed safe."

Reece grunted. "What was Redman's mission?"

"Rescue, non-lethal. We couldn't have done it better. No casualties, but no sign of the Dragon."

"Fine, let them walk. I'll be in touch with Redman later."

"Copy that."

Reece ended the call, just as the deputy director's assistant approached him.

"The deputy director will see you now," she said.

Reece braced himself for a major tongue lashing, and he wasn't disappointed.

"You want to tell me why you sent SWAT after Bishop and the girl?" the deputy director asked.

"We got a location—"

"The report I received makes a good case for the culprit being Maxwell and now you've received confirmation it was her weapon, not Bishop's, that fatally wounded Osborn. Why didn't you send SWAT after Maxwell?"

"I have no idea where she—"

"I don't want to hear your excuses. I just received a call from the York family attorney. They want to know who's paying for the damages to their twenty-million-dollar home?"

"It was a justified—"

"You will fix this HR nightmare before it gets anymore squirrelly. I don't want this department's news running on the front page, or Page Six. Have I made myself clear?"

"Yes, sir."

"And, do we have confirmation Bishop even knew he was being sought for questioning about a fellow agent's death?"

"No, sir."

"That's what I thought. So if I'm hearing things correctly, you agree that he was behaving as any agent would who was trying to protect a witness?" the deputy director said.

Reece was sure no one would believe that, but he had no desire to piss off the deputy director. "Understood."

"Good, now make this nightmare go away. Let me know when you find Maxwell."

"Yes, sir."

"You're dismissed."

Reece left the deputy director's office feeling only marginally better. At least now he had a plan. Bishop wouldn't be run through the wringer, but Reece was sure that had more to do with the possible backlash of negative publicity than it did with protecting Bishop.

42

BISHOP

Bishop was stuck in an interrogation room. Kat had been pulled away and taken to another location. No one was sharing any information with him. At least he wasn't handcuffed to the table, but the door was locked. He'd checked it. Thankfully, Redman's team rescued Rip. He'd heard that on the walkie-talkie before SWAT shut it all down.

Jayda was in the wind, but Bishop wasn't worried she'd return anytime soon. The city was too hot. She'd go to ground, as the assassin Evgeni had done after Haden's shooting.

Bishop had asked to see a lawyer, but so far nothing had come from it. They'd taken his burner phone and gun. They'd have taken his badge too if he'd had it on him, but as far as he knew that was still at the safe house.

Bishop had no legal leg to stand on. He'd purposefully avoided coming in because he knew they would arrest him for Jerry's murder. Maybe now they'd check his gun and clear him of that ridiculous charge.

Unless they somehow still believed part of Madeline's story, but according to Alex, Meghan had made a good case for Madeline being a traitor. If she stayed in the wind, they'd have no choice but to discount her testimony. It would never stand up in court.

The door to the interrogation room opened. It was ADIC Reece Patterson, Madeline's boss.

"I want a lawyer," Bishop said.

"It's your lucky day, son. You don't need one," Reece said.

Bishop wasn't sure how to respond. Had they checked his weapon that quickly?

"It has been brought to my attention that you were never informed that we were looking for you," Reece said. "We've also checked your service weapon. Apparently, there was some mix up in the paperwork. The slug that came out of agent Osborn isn't from your gun."

Bishop breathed a huge sigh of relief. He also saw this for what it was, a huge fucking get out of jail free card. Reece was basically saying Bishop couldn't have known he was wanted for questioning, therefore any actions he took not to come in were not intentional.

"Where are Kat and Rip?"

"Now the Rip situation is a different story. However, since I don't believe you make enough money to hire mercenaries, I'm going to assume that someone else orchestrated that entirely illegal rescue mission, and you knew nothing about it. Am I right?"

"Yes, sir." Bishop started to say something else, but Reece held up his hand to stop him.

"Patrick Redman and his team are claiming client privilege. I told them in the future that shit wouldn't work. But for this case and this case only I'm gonna let it slide."

Bishop again started to say something. Reece held up his hand again.

"There's no need to thank me. Because as far as I can tell, there's nothing going on that you would have needed to thank anyone for. Am I right?"

Bishop nodded his head.

"That's what I thought. Off the record—this has been one motherfucking clusterfuck. I don't like it when shit like this goes down in my neighborhood. Do you understand what I'm saying, son?" Reece asked.

"Yes, sir," Bishop said.

"Good. So it's not gonna be a surprise to you that a couple of my boys are gonna take you to the airport and put you on a plane to Chicago."

Bishop raised his hand to speak, but Reece shook his head.

"Do I need to repeat myself? Or are you going to get on that plane and go home?"

"Would it be—"

"I don't think you heard me, son. Is there going to be a problem with you getting on that plane and going home?"

Bishop knew when he was beaten. "No, sir."

"Good, good."

Bishop would call Kat once he got his phone replaced. The bureau had kept his burner phone. He couldn't argue with Reece about contacting Kat or all his good fortune could come back to bite him in the ass. For now, he had to get on that plane and sort things out from Chicago. Kat would understand—she had to. He knew she was safe—the FBI had nothing on her, and Bishop would make sure the locals knew she had nothing to do with the guy Jayda killed. Alex had probably already forwarded any evidence he'd found. And Kat could point out that there were two women in the bar that night wearing blue dresses.

It was clear from Reece's attitude that there was no way in hell he was going to get to stay in the city, or get an update on Kat, but maybe he'd share what he knew about Madeline.

"Any update on Madeline?" Bishop asked.

Reece gave him a pointed look but didn't answer his question. "The agents are ready to take you to the airport."

"Yes, sir."

A knock sounded on the door. Reece said, "Enter."

Two straight-faced veteran FBI agents stepped in the door. Neither looked like they ever gave any fucks. They would both do exactly what Reece said.

"You know what to do?" Reece asked.

They both nodded. The one on the right, who Bishop was going to call Blondie, dared to speak.

"The Chicago ADIC just got word about Malone. She made it through surgery. She's going to be fine."

"Good. Tough as nails, that one," Reece said. "Bishop, you might want to stay out of her way when she gets back to the office. She's dyed in the wool, an agent through and through."

Bishop nodded, but didn't say anything. What the fuck had happened to Meghan? He'd have to check in with Alex as soon as he replaced his phone.

"Now, if you'll excuse me, I have to go get my ass chewed out some more because I let SWAT loose on one of Vincent York's properties," Reece groused as he left Bishop in the hands of the other agents.

43

KAT

Kat paced the hospital room back and forth. No one was telling her anything. The FBI agents that took her from Vincent's house had taken her burner phone. There was a landline in the hospital room, but she didn't have Bishop's number. She knew Rip's number, but he'd left his phone at the apartment.

She wasn't even sure at this point why she was being held. The hospital had checked her over, taken blood to run additional tests, and asked if she needed anything. She hadn't, so that was it, but the FBI agent outside the door refused to let her leave. He'd said he needed permission to release her. She told him to call and ask, he ignored her. He was also no help about Bishop and Rip either. He refused to give her any information.

The door to Kat's room opened, but it was only Jasmine, the duty nurse. Jasmine was barely five foot but had the sweetest laugh of anyone Kat had ever met. She was the only reason Kat wasn't screaming to be released. The nurse's vivacious attitude put some of Kat's crazy life into perspective. It wasn't Jasmine's fault they were holding Kat at the hospital. She just wanted to go home, but she wouldn't get there any sooner by making the nurse's life difficult.

Kat tried to stay cheerful, but it wasn't easy. "Have you heard anything about Rip yet?" Kat asked.

Rip was alive, Kat had to believe that. Redman's team wouldn't have said they had the package if he'd been dead, right?

"No, I'm sorry," Jasmine said. "I haven't heard anything, but one of the other nurses said the police brought in a young guy that sounds like your roommate."

"Can I see him?"

"I'll ask, but I doubt it. I do have some good news," Jasmine grinned.

Kat's mood brightened. She hoped it wasn't an update on the flavor of Jell-O being served for dinner, because Kat wanted to be gone by then.

"All your lab work came back and everything is normal."

Kat tried not to be too disappointed that this was the good news. She'd not expected any results, assuming the hospital would send off her blood to be tested. But apparently they had procedures to follow, which included processing her blood work onsite. She was glad everything came back normal, but honestly, other than her stress level, which was through the roof, she hadn't expected anything to be abnormal.

"Any idea when I'll get to leave?" Kat asked.

Conspiratorially, Jasmine leaned in and whispered, "I've heard there's a detective here to speak with you but then after that you can go." Straightening back up she cleared her throat. In her normal voice, she said, "I haven't heard anything." Jasmine winked, making Kat smile.

Kat mouthed the words thank you. At least now she knew this ordeal was coming to an end. And hopefully the young guy Jasmine mentioned was Rip and she'd be reunited with him soon.

"Stay positive, Kat. We'll get you out of here in no time."

Jasmine left, leaving Kat to wonder exactly how long it would take the detective to show up.

Ten minutes later the door opened again. It was Jimmy Montgomery, the detective she'd met at the police station Sunday night. He had her purse. Kat took the bag and quickly checked its contents. No burner phone, but the envelope of cash was still there.

"Detective Montgomery, how are you?" Kat asked.

"This case has been a doozy, but I guess you know that," Montgomery said.

Kat nodded. Jasmine had said she could go after she talked with the detective. She also wasn't in handcuffs being interrogated at the station, so he clearly meant Kat would understand because she was connected to the case, not because he thought she was the killer. But they had shown up at her office to talk with her after watching the video, so it never hurt to ask.

"I assume you figured out I wasn't the woman with Mr. Smith at the restaurant Saturday?"

Montgomery nodded. "We have an APB out for the shooter. We spotted two women in blue on the tapes. We came down to your office to ask if you remembered seeing her at the restaurant."

"Then you got pulled into the intruder search," Kat offered.

"And the Greyson murder investigation. We haven't forgotten that you left the scene of the crime."

Kat hadn't considered that. She had no clue what the penalty was. Before she could ask, Montgomery continued.

"However, it is clear there were circumstances beyond your control."

"No kidding," Kat muttered.

"Once we had the photos of Greyson's killer, we made a match to the second woman at the restaurant."

"I also think she's who shot at me Sunday," Kat said.

Montgomery agreed. "Makes sense, but without a witness or a

confession, we may not be able to charge her with that crime. She'll go down for Greyson's murder, and we believe we have enough evidence to pin her with Smith's, as well."

"Do you have any leads on her whereabouts?" Kat asked.

"No."

"Is Rip here? Is he okay?" Kat asked.

"We've taken your roommate's statement. The hospital staff are finishing up with him now."

Kat was thankful Rip was safe, but that didn't help her anxiety about Bishop. "What about Bishop? FBI Special Agent Scott Bishop?" Kat asked.

"Apparently that's above my pay grade. The bureau put me in touch with one of their PR types, who refused to release any information."

"What does that mean?" Kat asked.

Montgomery shrugged. "The bureau is known for long debriefs."

Long debriefs. What the hell? Did that mean he was being charged for that other agent's murder?

"You can try calling the FBI switchboard, but don't hold your breath."

Kat nodded. "Yeah. I just wish I knew his status. One of the agents he worked with was killed. I hope he's been cleared."

"I can't say this is confirmation of that, but they rescinded Agent Bishop's APB and filed a new one for Madeline Maxwell," the detective said.

"That has to be good news, right?" Kat asked. If they took back the APB on Bishop he must no longer be a person of interest. Madeline Maxwell was his boss and the one running the op. That had to mean his name was cleared.

"Maybe," Montgomery said. "He's in custody, but normally an APB is just updated with capture details. Not sure you can call an all clear just yet."

Kat's shoulders slumped. Then she took a deep breath and shook off the bad vibes. Until she heard otherwise, she was assuming Bishop was safe and not being charged with a murder he didn't commit. Hopefully the FBI believed Madeline was the one that killed Osborn, which was why they issued the APB. Kat refused to believe differently.

"Thanks for the information, detective. Can you take me to Rip now?"

"Sure, follow me."

Her FBI guard was gone, which meant Kat wouldn't get another chance to ask about Bishop. He'd not told her anything anyway, so a tenth plea probably wouldn't have swayed him.

Montgomery led Kat down the hall toward another corridor. Her mood lifted when she heard Rip's voice.

"I can put on my own shirt," Rip said.

Kat practically knocked him over as she ran into his arms.

"Easy, Kit Kat. I just got rescued—by some super-hot commandos. You may need to baby me for a few days."

Kat could hear the humor in Rip's voice. She leaned back to get a better look at him. He had a few scrapes and bruises, but he was okay—alive. She didn't know what she would do if he hadn't come home.

Hugging him again, she said, "Don't scare me like that again, Rip. I mean it. I don't ever want to see another R-I-P note. Never again."

Rip's arms enveloped her. "Never again, Kit Kat. I promise."

Detective Montgomery cleared his throat. Kat and Rip separated.

"You're free to go, but we may need additional statements later," Montgomery said.

The detective nodded at Kat then turned to leave.

She looked back at Rip, tears in her eyes.

Rip wiped them away. "Hey, none of that. We made it. We

survived. Now, let's go find those commandos. I hear they were hired mercenaries—does that mean we can rent one?"

Kat knew Rip was joking, but she played along. "I think they may be out of our price range."

"We've still got the 3K right? How much can they cost? I mean if the police paid for them—"

"Oh, no. The police didn't pay for them." Kat remembered Rip wasn't up to speed about Bishop. "That is a much longer story. Let's get out of here and I'll tell you all about it. I actually need your help."

Rip took Kat's arm. "After you, madam."

As they left the hospital, Kat explained everything to Rip.

"So, you see, I sort of fell for Mr. Sexy," Kat said.

"Don't you mean Mr. Dangerous?" Rip asked.

"I don't know. Maybe Mr. Dangerously Sexy is what I need?" Kat winked at him.

"The guy that thought you were a hooker?"

Kat rolled her eyes. "It's more complicated than that. Anyway, he's really a super-hot FBI agent."

"That was wanted for murder."

"A misunderstanding—and now he's being debriefed by the FBI. But I don't know where he is."

"Kit Kat, is this guy really someone you want to tangle with?" Rip asked.

Kat looked into Rip's eyes. "It's crazy, I know, but yes. I want to see where this goes. I want to date him. I want to meet his family and friends. I want to hear about his day—I want to tell him about mine. I want to cuddle beside him on the couch while he watches sports and I read."

"He's a sports guy?" Rip asked.

"I don't know—but I want to find out."

"Does this mean we're moving to Chicago?" Rip asked.

Kat shrugged.

Rip pulled Kat in for a hug. "We'll make it work," he said, "but Kit Kat, I know drag queens and politicians, not FBI agents."

"You're so full of shit," she said, pulling away from him. "Your sister is married to a clerk of court and you've met one drag queen, once—and he wasn't even gay."

Rip raised his right eyebrow. "He was gay."

"Anyway, it doesn't matter. You are in fact uniquely qualified to help me find Bishop," she said.

"Really, do tell."

"First, we have to find Vincent York," Kat said.

Rip stopped, then turned to Kat. "Vincent-Fucking-York."

"Vincent-Fucking-York," Kat confirmed. "And don't pretend you don't know exactly where your man crush is right now. Because we both know you have been drooling after his fine ass since he sashayed back to civilization and threw a giant, I'm-king-of-the-fucking-world-and-don't-forget-it bash."

Rip smiled. "Okay, so he might be in the city—at his club, that you didn't take me to."

Kat started to argue, but Rip held up his hand.

"It was a rumor I heard from clingy Asian guy before I got kidnapped, but I'm sure it's legit."

Thank God for clingy Asian guys. "Okay, so how do we talk to him?"

Kat stepped out to the curb, ready to hail a taxi.

"You can't just show up at his club," Rip said. "We'd have better luck at his hotel."

Kat clapped her hands together. "Yay! But only if you're up for it."

"I'm always up for Vincent York."

"Ugh, gross," Kat said, slapping him on the chest. "He's not gay."

Rip clutched his heart as if Kat had wounded him. "Not yet," he said, giving her a wink.

Kat knew Rip would freeze when he came face to face with York, but until then he'd be the wingman she needed to get past security and meet the man himself. He had to help her find Bishop. He was Vincent-Fucking-York after all, which according to Rip meant he could do anything.

44

RYKER

Ryker wasted no time leaving New York City after Greyson's death. As soon as he received word that Ana had left for London, he chartered a plane. Now he was in the UK, instead of stuck in the middle of an inept FBI investigation. Ryker had no intention of ever dealing with the crazy FBI bitch again. She'd been on a major power trip. Ryker wasn't sure how Bishop dealt with it. He'd claimed to be one of General Davis's boys. Ryker requested Bishop's details be sent to him so he could review the files while he was on the plane.

According to the files he'd read, Scott Bishop was one of the four men the Army Rangers decided to sacrifice for the greater good. That mission was part of the reason Ryker worked for the CIA. If the Rangers could railroad dedicated soldiers like Bishop and his crew, what chance did Ryker have to make it out alive?

Recently the general had gotten new information—the kind to finally clear the names of the four men they'd almost destroyed. Davis would now be able to take out the Ortega cartel, or at least significantly diminish its influence.

Ryker's handlers weren't happy about that. Too much change in an area could destabilize it. Removing the Ortega cartel too quickly, without identifying who would fill the power vacuum, was a dangerous plan. Ryker didn't begrudge Davis or his men the closure they deserved, but the wrong bad guy in a position of power could jeopardize the world.

Ryker was in London to end Ana Ivanov. Nick needed his sister dead if he was going to take over the Ivanov clan. Ryker's handlers wanted her dead so Nick could take the throne. Ana was prone to reckless business decisions, which wasn't a good skill to have for the leader of the third largest oligarch family in Russia. Ryker's CIA handlers believed Nick would do a much better job managing the family's businesses.

Mikhail had been a fool to disown his son. Ana never had the right temperament to run her father's empire, but after tonight none of that would matter. Nick would run the Ivanov clan and the world would be a tiny bit safer.

Ryker had stopped at his hotel and changed. He had to play the part. Everything about his look, from his gold and diamond cufflinks, to his $10,000 watch, to his bespoke suit and $2,000 Italian loafers, screamed money. Considering Ryker had grown up in Texas as a military brat, and joined the army right out of high school, he never expected to find himself being anything other than a soldier. But Uncle Sam didn't only need soldiers. Sometimes he needed killers.

Ryker took a taxi to the bar. He spotted Ana as soon as he walked in. She was sitting off to the side in a small alcove schmoozing with an octogenarian in a tailored suit. The guy looked old enough to be her grandfather and his demeanor looked stuffy. He was probably an accountant or realtor for the wealthy Dukes and Duchesses of British society. A man with connections and respectability. A man just like Greyson and Koshy.

Ryker scanned the bar area. Ana didn't go anywhere without her protection. Ryker spotted a goon chatting up one of the servers. Ryker checked the bar again, but he was the only one.

Ana's protection detail was light tonight—good. That meant there would be less people to kill.

Ryker nodded to the bartender and motioned to Ana's bodyguard, who was standing at the bar. The bartender, an operative Ryker had worked with before, gave an almost imperceptible nod before taking out a special bottle from underneath the counter. He poured a shot, then took it over to the chatty bodyguard. The bartender pointed toward a group of women who appeared to be celebrating one of their group's last nights of freedom, a hen party—or bachelorette party in the States. They were all drunk off their asses and not paying attention to the bartender as he implied they'd paid for the shot he was delivering to the bodyguard. The goon gave a small smile as if he couldn't believe his luck. He took the shot holding it up to the ladies and nodded. They giggled in drunken bliss as they saw him for the first time.

Without missing a beat, the bodyguard knocked the shot back then slammed the glass on the bar. Swaying a bit, he grabbed onto the edge of the bar for support. Shaking his head, as if trying to clear his vision, his legs became unsteady.

The server helped the bodyguard fall into a seat at the bar, guiding his head down as if he'd passed out. The bartender passed a few dollars to the server, who walked away to take another order. The bartender made sure Ryker saw the bodyguard. The shot would keep the bodyguard unconscious for at least two hours, plenty of time for Ryker to do his job.

From the shadows, Ryker watched Ana. She was too focused on her new recruit to notice that her protection was slumped over the bar unconscious. Ana wasn't going to be so lucky. She wouldn't get to walk out of here tonight. Her days running roughshod over everyone else were over. The sad part of it was that if the CIA thought she could run the Ivanovs better than Nick, Ryker would be taking out Nick instead of Ana. But they didn't. The CIA knew Ana could never fill her father's shoes.

Ryker clumsily made his way over to Ana's alcove, sliding in beside her.

"I'm sorry, sir, but the seat is taken," Ana said, obviously not recognizing him.

In a drunken Texas twang, he said, "Come on, baby, you know you want some of this."

Ryker grabbed Ana's thigh, injecting her with a small amount of a very lethal poison.

"Ow. Take your hands off me," Ana yelled.

"I'm sorry, good sir," Ana's mark said, "but you need to leave the lady alone."

Ryker made an exaggerated gesture, as he removed his hand from Ana's thigh. "I'm sorry. My bad."

Ana pushed his hand away. "How dare you. Where is my guard?" Looking down at her leg, she saw a small dot of blood. "You bastard, you cut me."

Ryker met Ana's eyes and gave her a knowing look.

"You son of bitch," Ana screamed.

Ryker chuckled. "Don't worry, darlin', I didn't mean nothin' by it." Ryker made eye contact with the mark. "I'll leave you to it then."

The man looked offended and startled, as only the British could.

Ryker got up, stumbling a bit for show, and quickly left the bar. He could hear Ana behind him yelling for her guard. Then she started coughing. He knew what would happen next. He didn't need to watch. He'd read about it in the paper tomorrow.

Taking out his phone, Ryker brought up the texting app. He selected Nick from his contacts.

RYKER: It's done

45

KAT

Kat was on her way to the airport, where Bishop was waiting to fly back to Chicago, which meant he hadn't been arrested.

"My offer still stands, babe. I'm here for you." Rip's wonderful voice came through her phone. He was across town at the Four Seasons.

This was the same thing he'd said the night she met Bishop.

Kat knew Rip meant it, and not just because they'd had the most horrible few days of their lives and survived. Rip was Kat's best friend and he always would be.

"Don't get used to that posh living—you've got to go back to the real world soon," Kat said.

"My boy Vincent York totally hooked me up with this fine pad for three days—and you're one to talk Miss I'm-On-My-Way-To-The-Airport-To-Fly-First-Class-To-Chicago courtesy of the same Vincent York."

Rip was right—they were both getting a small reprieve from reality. Him to forget what Jayda had done to him, and her to chase a dream that might not be real. Vincent York had come through in the most amazing way—no thanks to Rip, who could barely string two words together. Kat had to jump in and beg for Vincent's help to find Bishop, before Rip got them both tossed out of the hotel.

"Do you think I'm doing the right thing?" Kat asked.

Rip paused, a little longer than Kat would have liked. "His job is dangerous, Kit Kat, but I think you've got to try. Nobody's perfect."

Bishop's job was dangerous, but nothing worth having was easy. She wanted the passion they shared to be real. She wanted to be held in his arms every night until she fell asleep. She wanted him. It was that simple. She wanted Scott Bishop to belong to her.

"I want this," Kat said.

"You deserve this," Rip said.

"Thanks, babe. I'll see you in a few days."

Kat hung up, dropping her phone back in her bag. She'd just arrived at the airport. She had nothing with her except her purse. Like Rip, she'd had no desire to return to her apartment tonight and once she knew Bishop was at the airport, her path was simple. Vincent just made it easy. He bought two tickets in first class. One for Bishop, who was flying coach thanks to the FBI, and the other for her.

Kat checked in, got her boarding pass, and headed for the gate.

Unfortunately, Bishop wasn't there. Unsure what to do, she went to the counter.

"Excuse me, has Scott Bishop checked in?" Kat asked.

"If he's not here, then no," a grumpy middle-aged attendant said.

A younger, slightly less harried attendant interrupted. "Check the first class lounge," she said, pointing toward a door on the other side of the corridor.

"Thanks," Kat said.

Turning toward the first class lounge, Kat took in a deep

breath. Dangerous, unpredictable, Scott Bishop was the guy for her. For him, she'd even consider skydiving. Which didn't mean she'd go, but contemplating jumping out of a perfectly good airplane for the man you might love counted, right?

Laughing at herself, she headed for the lounge.

BISHOP

Bishop and his two bodyguards/babysitters were sitting in the first class lounge across from his gate. Their tickets were coach, but the FBI had an arrangement with the airport to allow access to the lounge for non-felon protection details. He had no way to contact Kat. The FBI had taken his burner phone and neither agent seemed willing to stop by a store on the way to the airport for Bishop to get a replacement. It wasn't like he had her number anyway, but with a phone he could have started making calls. Someone had to have her details, or at least an update. Bishop trusted that Kat was safe. He just wanted to know for sure.

Bishop hated feeling lost. He wanted to know where Kat was. He wanted to tell her to wait for him. He didn't know how he was going to make it work, because there was no way in hell Reece would let him transfer to NYC, but he would make it work. If Kat was in New York, then that's exactly where Bishop wanted to be too.

The FBI wasn't Bishop's only option. There were plenty of jobs he could do. Especially in New York.

Bishop looked up to check the time on the clock above the

receptionist. That was when he saw her. It took him a minute to realize what he was looking at.

It was Kat.

How the hell had she found him?

Bishop jumped up, startling the other agents. He didn't care if they tried to tackle him to the ground, nothing was going to stop him from holding Kat in his arms. She must've had the same thought because as soon as their eyes locked she ran toward him. They crossed the small distance, slamming their bodies together in a powerful hug.

Bishop squeezed her tight. "Ohmygod, you're safe, thank God you're safe," Bishop said, breathing in Kat's unique smell. He still couldn't believe this was real. "I couldn't get away. I had no phone. I didn't know your number."

"Shhh..." Kat said. "It's okay. I'm here now, thanks to your friend, Vincent York—who has some scary mad skills when it comes to getting information from the FBI."

Bishop laughed, pushing Kat back to look at her. His eyes roved over her body, making sure she was whole and unhurt.

Bishop wiped a single tear from Kat's cheek. "I didn't want to leave without—"

Kat put a finger over Bishop's lips. "I don't want to lose this thing we have. I want to see where this is going. I want to date and make love and meet each other's parents. I want to hang out and know if you're a sports guy or a gamer or both. I want to explore options. I have nothing tying me to New York City—and Rip even hinted he'd move with me. I want us to take a shot at this—if you want to."

Bishop couldn't believe it. He'd not considered she'd be willing to move. "I would love the chance to get to know you. I want to explore what we have—without all the someone-is-trying-to-kill-us drama."

"Deal," she said. "As long as you don't mind my baggage—Rip will grow on you, I promise."

Bishop smiled. "Mr. Sexy can live with that."

Kat laughed. "Should we have a Red Martini to celebrate?"

"Oh, no. If I let you near one of those we'll probably wind up with frequent flyer points in the Mile High Club."

Kat raised her right eyebrow. "Mr. Sexy, what makes you think that won't happen either way?"

"Come here, beautiful. I don't think I've kissed you enough today," Bishop said, pulling Kat in for the first kiss of the rest of their lives.

The End

ABOUT THE AUTHOR

Sloane Savage is a software developer by day and an author of action packed Romantic Suspense at night. She grew up in South Carolina, but has called the Sunshine State home since 1997. She has a master's degree in Computer Science, but her love of writing has really unleashed the creative siren in her soul.

For the latest information, visit Sloane's website at http://sloanesavage.com

facebook.com/SloaneSavageAuthor
twitter.com/SavageReads
instagram.com/sloanesavage

THANK YOU

If you enjoyed this book, please consider leaving a review.

Made in the USA
Columbia, SC
08 January 2023